DEVON

Devon

Dria Andersen

Adrienne Andersen

Author's Note

So, we're starting a new series with a brand new pair of brothers and I'm excited, I hope you are too. It's set in the same world as the Knight brothers, so some of the characters that you love will make their appearances.

Content Warnings:

Cursing, violence, gun violence, explicit sex, mentions of cheating and drug dealing.

Dedication

To my husband, who is my sounding board, my cheerleader, my critique partner, and all the things I needed to finish this, and every project I've worked on. I appreciate every hour, every word of input, and, most of all, your unwavering support.

To my family, who had to deal with mommy being in another world for hours at a time. Thank you for being so patient.

To my aunt Cathy who gave me my first love of romance stories, I thank you for allowing me to raid your bookshelf.

Thank you to every fan who continues to stick with me while telling the stories playing in my head. I appreciate each and every one of you. A special thanks to Shirelle and Rayshawnda for being my sounding boards and amazing Beta readers. I would like to give thanks to A.K Edits for editing and polishing my words.

1...

Devon took his first free breath after ten years. He closed his eyes against the bright sun and tilted his head back. Fuck! The heat against his face felt amazing. He rounded his shoulders and lowered his head, opening his eyes at the same time the very last gate opened to release him back into the world. For a moment, his steps faltered, an ingrained fear from his years inside. He approached the gate slowly at first, his steps eventually picking up as he neared it.

Save the employee cars, the parking lot was nearly deserted except for an SUV idling a few feet away from him. The vehicle was black, the tint on the windows just as dark, until not even shadows could be seen behind the glass. The door opened, and the smile on his face widened as his baby brother stepped out clean as fuck in a pair of slacks. His dress shirt was rolled up to his elbows and his tie was loose at his neck.

He and Declan looked alike despite their years apart, from the same chestnut brown skin and dark brown almond-shaped eyes down to their strong chins. Devon's was currently covered in a heavy beard in need of trimming where Declan's beard was close to his skin and shaved down neatly. His brother's hair was low, closed to his head, waves along the top and tapered sharply on the sides. Declan's face had filled out in the ten years they'd been apart, and now, the two brothers were nearly identical.

A lot had changed in the years he'd been locked up. Gone was the teenager he'd fought to keep out of the streets. In his place was a grown ass man.

"Baby boy," he called out, rushing toward his brother.

Declan made quick feet to meet him, throwing his arms around him.

They held tight before separating and butting heads together. Their shoulders grazed as Devon pulled his baby brother's head closer to slide his cheek against his to greet his animal. If they were not outside of a prison, the greeting would more likely devolve into slap boxing. It was the way wolves communicated, the rough-housing a part of their tactile nature. After so many years physically apart, both animals and humans were starved of their familiar affection. Pulling Devon in tighter, Declan growled lowly, his wolf asserting its pleasure at finally being connected to his brother.

"My motherfucker out!" Declan said gruffly.

Devon stepped back. "You look good."

"Shit." Declan's face was painted in emotions.

"None of that shit," Devon chided him, his voice thick with his own emotion. He nodded toward the Bentley. "You came stepping, ain't it?"

Dec chuckled. "Nothing but the best for my big brother."

"Yes, sir," he said, rubbing his hands together. "I'm hungry than a bitch, let's get out of here."

Devon turned and gave one final look to the prison that had held him during his most formative years. The only way he was coming back was in a pine box, he swore to himself. He followed his brother into the truck, sighing as cold air enveloped him. He'd barely buckled his seat belt before the driver took off.

He nodded to the front seat. "You riding with security now?"

"I handle money for some people that like to make sure they shit safe," Declan told him.

Devon nodded because he understood that. "Plus, the moves you trying to make."

Declan smiled at him. "We got a few meetings about that."

"We?" he teased.

"I waited on you. I don't move without you at my side."

Devon's heart warmed. "I'm proud of you, Dec." It wasn't the first or even eighth time he'd told his brother that. He made sure that Declan knew how much he valued what he did every time they talked over the phone.

Declan passed him a phone box. "I know it ain't the flip phone you're used to."

Devon laughed. "Fuck you."

His brother smirked at him. Devon powered it on, and a moment later, a video call came through. He smiled because it was a group call. As soon as he answered, four little squares popped up.

"A motherfucker is free," Silas said with a big smile.

"How that air taste?" Julian asked.

He cracked up. "I know y'all missed me."

"Shit, I talked to you more inside than I did when you were out," Mason grumbled.

Declan snickered. It was probably true for all of them. Though the walls had held him in place, it hadn't stopped him from running the various businesses he'd had on the outside. He'd had to count on his brother a lot, as well as his friends. There were a few people that worked for him, but his trust didn't extend to too many outside of the group he was speaking with.

"What's the move?" Rocco asked.

Devon looked at his brother. Declan smiled but said nothing, which meant he was up to something.

"Shit, let me get to town and settle in, then I'll hit y'all up."

"Bet," Silas said.

Declan shook his head. "They mated now. Y'all ain't finna do nothing but rock in some chairs on the porch."

Devon hollered.

"Always on bullshit," Silas said, laughing.

"Ol' jealous ass," Julian chimed in.

"Ain't nobody jealous. I can go see some titties right now if I wanted to," Declan joked.

They all cracked up.

"Hit us up and we'll come over to see the house," Rocco said. "I ain't trying to be in the streets anyway."

"That ain't new," he teased Rocco, mouthing, 'New house?' to Declan. His brother smiled.

Devon looked up as the car slowed down. His eyebrows winged in surprise as they were escorted through the gate of a private airstrip. He stared at the large hangar bays that stored various aircraft. He was in disbelief as they pulled up to a small, sleek silver plane already idling on the runway. Stairs descended onto the asphalt of the tarmac and a flight attendant stood waiting for them at the top.

"I'll send y'all the address," Declan told the group. "We gotta catch this flight, so be easy."

"A'ight, fam. Congrats again," Julian told him.

The others repeated the sentiment and hung up the call. Devon stared at his brother as the driver got out the truck and grabbed bags from the back.

Declan smiled. "I told you I was flipping your shit. You thought I was joking?"

"You went way past flipping if we got private jet money," Devon said in surprise.

Declan snorted. "It belongs to one of my clients, even though I told him renting was more fiscally responsible."

Devon knew that the money he'd made slinging had been washed by his brother and converted into legitimate income streams, but this… He was not expecting anything like this. He assumed he'd come out and be comfortable, but Bentley trucks and private jets?

Shit.

He kept his composure as he entered the jet. The interior was spacious, but what most caught his attention were the brown bags on the table between two plush leather seats. The logo for Ms. B's was on the bags, and his stomach grumbled in response. His little brother had thought of everything.

"Ms. B's still open?" he asked, working to contain his emotions.

"Yep, thanks to you," Devon answered absently as he sat in the seat.

"Me?" Devon looked toward the back and the other tables and seats on the plane.

"One of your many investments," his brother told him. Declan nodded toward the bags the driver had placed in the seat across the aisle from him. "There's clothes and shit in there, and a shower in the back. Flight's about an hour."

Devon wiped a hand down his face, shocked but so proud of his brother. While he'd been in prison still hustling to take care of their family, his brother had been outside doing even more.

"Dec," he whispered.

His brother nodded, his eyes wet. "Yeah, we can talk about all that shit when we get you home."

There was nothing else to say, so Devon grabbed the bag, happy to get out of prison clothes and truly clean.

2...

She blinked against the glaring sun as she departed the small jet. Her boss only traveled private, and today, she was very happy for that. Her head was pounding, her wolf damn near slipping from her control. She realized that it had been a few weeks since she'd shifted. The animal was restless, and in her tired state, getting control was harder than normal. Keisha's chest rumbled as she slid into the waiting SUV. Rocco quirked an eyebrow at she passed him leaning against the truck, on the phone. He and her boss were talking in a group call.

She waved off his concern.

As soon as they got home, she would sleep a day and then head to Washington Park for some much-needed time in her wolf form. She'd call her mother to accompany her. Keisha loved when they spent time there, and she needed to touch base with Patrice. It felt like she'd been running on fumes for months, and time with her mother tended to refresh her. Something about the woman's energy soothed her wolf like nothing else.

Silas Knight slid into the back seat, finished with his phone call. He sighed and leaned his head back against the headrest, closing his eyes. She could see his exhaustion all over his face. She was sure it mirrored her own.

"The session is over," she offered.

He scoffed. "I swear they're getting longer."

"You ain't lying," Rock spoke up from the front.

"Your Monday is light if that helps. Just a couple of meetings to go over the legislature that passed this session." She pulled out her tablet from her messenger bag to confirm even though she knew his schedule like the back of her hand.

Silas put a hand over hers to prevent her from opening the tablet case. "Please, Keisha, rest. That shit can wait until next week."

"I have every intention of resting the entire weekend," she assured him.

"Matter of fact, move the meetings to Wednesday and we'll take a long weekend." He must've sensed their incredulous stares because his eyes popped opened. "What?"

Rock snickered.

"I rest," he argued. "Move the meetings, ma. I'm tired as hell, and I miss my babies."

She didn't wait on him to say it again, quickly sending off messages to the office they had in DC to move their meetings back to Wednesday after lunch.

"I don't even know what I'ma do with four days in a row off," she murmured more to herself.

Silas chuckled. "You bet not let Ms. Patrice hear you say that. I'm sure she can find something for you to do."

She snorted. He was right about that. Her mother did not believe in idle hands.

He sat forward and pulled his phone from his jacket pocket. "Mila has this resort she and Celine go to when they need a weekend away from the kids. It's on the beach."

Her interest was piqued. Her wolf loved the water as much as the woman did.

"Hold on." He called his wife. "Hey, love."

His voice softened, and Keisha sighed. She wanted that so bad. But between her work schedule and her very exacting standards, finding a man was proving impossible. A part of her longed to have someone care for her the way he cared for his mate. Observing him as well as Rocco and his mate Julissa, she'd seen firsthand how it could be to have someone fully invest in another person. She wanted that for herself, but some part of her held back when it came to men. Her therapist would point it squarely back to the relationship she had with her mother and Patrice's relationship with her father.

But...she wasn't in the mood to delve into that. She tuned back into his conversation when she heard her name. Silas told his mate he would call her back, and she held her breath as he turned to her.

"Mila is making a reservation for you."

"Silas," she protested in surprise.

He held up his hand to stall her words. "It's the least I can do for how well you take care of me and the office. It's for tonight until Tuesday. Relax and let someone take care of you for once."

His words were harmless but along the same lines of what she'd just been thinking, so they sank into her, making her a little more restless than she'd been minutes ago. She nodded, knowing arguing with her boss would be useless.

Keisha stood at the window of the lavish suite Mila had booked for her. It was decorated in soft, soothing creams and whites. The king-sized bed looked plush, the down blanket on top inviting her to dive under. There was a sitting area in the other room, separated by a reed divider that filtered the light, making the whole scene serene.

Everything had been paid for, including anything she needed to add to the room's tab. Mila had even booked a couple of appointments at the spa located within the hotel. It was the definition of luxurious, and Keisha looked forward to being pampered. The whole resort was shifter-friendly, so despite the delicate touches, the furniture was made to withstand and accommodate any size animal their patrons shifted into. The windows were large and took up most of the wall, but not even the roar of the waves from the beach below penetrated the silence of the room.

Keisha was excited about that most of all. She talked and listened to people all day at work; she was anxious for the quiet.

It had taken her an hour to shower at home and repack a bag for the weekend. The resort was only forty minutes from her apartment, so she'd arrived well before dusk. She'd put on a simple pair of biker shorts and a sports bra because her intention had been to strip and jump into the bed when she arrived, but Keisha had made the mistake of calling her mother after she'd settled into the room. Sighing, she turned from the darkening view of the ocean.

"I'm not home, mama," she said, going back to the conversation they were having.

"I thought y'all were back today."

"I'm in the city, but Mr. Knight and his wife booked me a room at this resort."

"Oh, fancy!" her mother exclaimed. "Good, it's good he shows his appreciation."

She chuckled. "Trust me, he pays me well for my hours."

"Okay, well, I'll leave you alone to relax. Besides, Benny can do with a couple of days in lockup."

Keisha sighed at the reminder of why their conversation had gone on for so long. Her mother had been trying to convince her that they should help her cousin.

"Mama, you can't save them all."

"I know, but Mel asked, and I figured it couldn't hurt to ask you."

Keisha put the phone on speaker on the dresser so she could massage her temples. "Mama, you can't let them take advantage of you. Aunt Mel lets his ass get away with too much as it is."

Her aunt Melanie was her father's sister, and ever since he'd passed nearly ten years ago, the family had been using her mother's good heart to take advantage. First with the money her father had left, and when that was gone, they took advantage of Patrice's time. Her mother was sweet and naïve despite the shit her mate used to get into, and Keisha could never understand how the woman kept herself from being jaded. That was another topic her and her therapist had discussed in detail.

Keisha wished her mother had moved back to the South side of Eastfield so they could've been close to her family versus staying on the West side within the clutches of her father's family. But Patrice had insisted that Keisha be brought up with wolves since she was one. Her mother hadn't wanted her to be the odd one out amongst the panthers in her family. Keisha loved her mother's side of the family, so she'd never understood that.

"You can't keep rescuing him every time he gets into trouble," she continued. "What does she expect me to do?"

"She thought you could maybe call in some favors."

Keisha sucked her teeth. "Chile."

Why her father's family thought her boss's contacts extended to her, she'd never know. There was no way she was asking Silas for anything for them so they could turn around and make her look like Boo Boo the fool.

Patrice chuckled. "It's why she called me and not you."

"Because she knew I would've told her off...respectfully," Keisha added hastily.

Patrice sighed.

"Mama, daddy's gone, and you do what you can for his family, but they take gross advantage of you. I worry about you."

"That's not your job, love," her mama gently chided. "Let me go. She'll probably try and call you anyway. Do not answer, hear me?"

"That ain't no problem because I wasn't gon' do that anyway." Unlike her mother, Keisha paid her father's family dust when it came to putting up with their foolishness. She helped the cousins that would appreciate it when she could, but the rest? She left them where they were. It had taken years of work to establish her boundaries, and she was not budging on them.

"I love you." She could hear the smile in Patrice's voice.

"I love you too, mama." And she did. It was for Patrice that she often stretched herself thin fooling with the Calhouns.

"Call me when you get back Tuesday."

"I'll call you before then." She rolled her eyes. She and her mother talked every day, she didn't know why the woman was tripping. "I need to make sure you managed to stay out of trouble."

They laughed and hung up. Keisha sighed, glancing at the giant king-sized bed. She would order room service and read, just like she'd planned to do when she got home. The only difference was the setting. She smiled, finally ready to relax. She couldn't wait to see the rest of the resort tomorrow.

3...

Devon could admit to being a little overwhelmed as he glanced out the wide window and patio doors of his new living room. The whole bottom level was open-concept, with the kitchen and living area facing the back of the house and a beautiful view of the beach on the other side of his pool. His brother had explained that the glass was manufactured to withstand the hurricane-force winds that came with living in Florida. It all took his breath away.

The whole room was white, with overlarge furniture in deep teal and calming blues. The floors were tiled and cool beneath his feet as he stood at the kitchen sink. He loved the fact that even though he had neighbors, they were spaced enough not to be a bother. His house was set far off from the main road, with its own utility road leading up to a gated entrance. It felt private and was the perfect place to reintroduce himself into society.

His brother couldn't have chosen a better place.

Devon yawned again, shaking off the nap that had lasted way too long. He knew it would take him forever to get to sleep tonight, but it was probably for the best. He imagined it would take a few days to adjust to being free. The amount of space in the five-bedroom beach house was likely too much after being confined for so long, but his wolf could stretch, and that was a blessing.

A part of him knew he should relax, but he was already making a list of shit he needed to do next week. He'd promised his brother the weekend, but after that, there was money to get and people to link up with. He eyed the phone on his counter as it rang. Speaking of…

"What it do, Tangie?"

She breathed out, quiet for a moment, and Devon already knew her overly sensitive ass was trying not to cry. He chuckled, and she sucked her teeth.

"Come open the door," she snapped, her voice clear.

Devon smiled and headed for the heavy, oversized front door. He pulled it opened and spotted the only person other than his little brother that he would do time for. She rushed into his arms immediately, her petite body settling into his larger one.

"You're late," he rumbled.

She gave him a watery laugh. "Whatever. Are you settling in okay?" He led her into the kitchen, and her eyes took in the house. "Declan did his big one with this house."

"Right?" Devon commented. "How you been?"

"I talked to you yesterday," she pointed out dryly.

"You the one over there crying like you ain't talk to me every day."

Tangie rolled her eyes and waved him off. Her sandy brown hair was pulled into a puff at the top of her head, the freckles across her caramel-colored nose standing out since she wasn't wearing makeup. She'd hated them when they were teenagers, which was the last time he'd seen her without a plexiglass partition between them. If he were human, perhaps they could've met in a common room like most prisons, but they were a lot more careful with shifters, restricting them even more than most federal prisoners.

"I'm glad you're free," she said softly.

"I told you about blaming yourself, Tangie. We were all into dumb shit. I was bound to be caught."

"I should've taken the charge," she said with tears in her eyes.

He held up his hand to stop her. "I'm not having this argument with you again. Besides, you damn near did the ride with me."

Tangie had visited him often and called him every day. Whether or not it was guilt that prodded the action, he'd still appreciated it.

She nodded and dropped it. "Where's Declan?"

"Working in the office somewhere down here," he replied, pulling dinner fixings from the refrigerator. "You staying?"

"No. I came to put eyes on you, then I'm going to pick up my son," she told him. "I did want to talk to you, but that can wait."

Devon tilted his head in curiosity.

Tangie shook her head. "Later. I don't want to interrupt your time with your brother."

He dropped it for now. Devon knew that guilt was a big part of his relationship with Tangie; he just hoped she would finally let it go now that he was out. She blamed herself for him going to jail, but in the end, he would have rather suffered than allowed her to. Especially since she'd been pregnant at the time. His mother had lost her life giving birth to Declan while she was behind bars. He would never wish that on another woman, especially one he was close friends with. She'd made a mistake in who she trusted, but Devon wouldn't let her pay for that.

"Wow, Tangie. It's been what, fifty years since I last saw you?" Declan called as he came into the kitchen, carrying his laptop.

Tangie snorted and accepted a sideways hug from his brother. "I'm headed out. I just wanted to see for myself that he was out."

Devon walked her to the door, dropping a kiss to the top of her head. "Quit stressing, woman."

She laughed and shook her head, then wrapped her arms around his waist and held him tight a moment before releasing him. "Call me when you figure out what you're doing in this free state of yours."

He nodded and waited until she was in her car and pulling off before he closed the door. His brother was at the island in his kitchen, tapping away at his laptop.

"You hungry?"

"That's why I came out the office," Declan answered. He gave his brother his full attention. "You like the house?"

"Shit's sweet," Devon told him, pulling out the beef he'd taken out earlier to thaw. "Plus, the fridge was stocked, so I'm more than satisfied."

He sliced meat in silence while his brother worked, content to be in the same space with Declan after so many years apart. They had so much to catch up on.

"Talk to me, baby brother," he said as he continued to prep dinner.

"Shit. Building," Declan answered. "Our jits will never go through what we went through."

"That's what's up. I noticed the workshop," he commented with a smile.

Declan returned it with a lopsided one of his own. "I would've never thought you'd flip prison vocational training into money like that. Now you can tinker without anyone standing over your shoulder."

One of the issues Devon thought he would have was deciding what he would do once he got out of prison. It was a common problem. But now, he had options, and he had his brother to thank for removing the temptation of easy money. Though Devon still had ties to the street crew he'd been in when he was locked up, it was time for him to give that up — especially in light of the plans his brother had.

"Tell me about your plans."

Declan sighed. "You know how the West side felt when we were growing up, but it's getting worse. Since Leland was killed and you were knocked, there was a vacuum."

Devon nodded in understanding. There was only so much he could control from behind bars.

"I'm not saying the boys under you not doing what they're supposed to do, but the Motsi moved in to fill that vacuum. Promising people shit they didn't deliver, taking a percentage of the money moving through the neighborhood." Declan sighed. "You know what happens when people get desperate."

Devon cursed. "Why didn't you tell me?"

"For you to do what? Your crew did what they could, fed who they could, but Cyrus... That greedy motherfucker has his foot on the whole neighborhood's neck. You should see how full the shelters are."

He frowned. "He been in your business?"

Despite trying to keep his brother out of trouble, Declan used his financial institution to wash money for some of the biggest gangsters on this side of the country.

"Nah, he wish he could touch me," Declan scoffed.

"So what you wanna do?"

"Now that you're out, we got a meeting with Mr. D tomorrow evening."

His eyebrow raised. "He in?"

"He approached me," Declan told him.

That made Devon feel better about the whole thing. If Dallas Knight was backing his brother, then it was as good as done. He started mentally moving stuff around to facilitate his and Declan's future. It meant that being in the streets like he was before was dead. There couldn't be anything that would disqualify Declan from holding the council position, though he didn't think that would matter. The tri-council was the governing body for all of the shifters in Eastfield, consisting of one representative of each of the shifter branches. Dallas Knight stood for the feline shifters who resided on the South side of town, while Micah Crespo was the Ursa representative over the East side. Currently, Cyrus Booth controlled the Lupine shifters on the West side. That was the position Declan wanted, and Devon would do everything in his power to deliver it to him.

Getting the council seat would be bloody and messy, but it was nothing new to either brother. It would change their circumstances even more. The Motsi society was comprised of the richest, most powerful shifters in the city, and Declan getting that seat would put them smack dab in the middle of it. It would be a whole new way of life, but if he could adapt to the rough life in the streets, this should be easy shit.

"Okay, so we're doing this."

Declan nodded. "We're doing this."

4...

His wolf nosed around the shells scattered amongst the sand in the back of his house. He'd been in his animal form for the last three hours, running up and down the beach, enjoying his freedom. While in jail, shifting had been a luxury only allowed twice a month and under strict watch. He'd remembered it being different in the juvenile prison he'd been in the first time he got knocked. The federal prison he'd found himself in as an adult took a different approach to shifters.

They were heavily monitored, going so far as to make them wear collars around their arms that not only prevented them from shifting but quelled their animal until it became a docile presence in the back of their consciousness. It had taken Devon a couple of years to teach himself and his wolf how to remain united under those conditions. The suppression usually caused the shifters to lose touch with their animals completely. His meditations had made for better control of Devon's wolf, and it also prevented the madness that beset a lot of the prisoners.

He could still hear the screams when he closed his eyes.

When he'd shifted this afternoon, it had still taken some coaxing from him to his wolf. The animal was used to running in circles in the four hundred square feet enclosure where they'd allowed the shifters to run. But once the wolf had gotten that first taste of fresh air, he'd taken off, inhibitions dropped. Now, three hours into his animal form, they were both tired. Dusk was falling, the night bringing a slight chill with it. Devon padded up to his discarded shorts, tiredly changing his form.

He slid the ball shorts up his legs and walked the few feet directly to the edge of the water.

He flopped down, propping his arms on his legs, taking in the ocean. He allowed the salt-tinged air to soothe him, the last rays of the sun pressing against his skin. His brother couldn't have picked a better place for him. He would've been content to live in their old neighborhood, but this? It felt like a freedom he would've never attained. He'd been making money before he went to jail, but to the extent Declan had flipped it…

He could only shake his head. His brother was smart as fuck, and it was one of the reasons Devon had been so careful to shield him from his own actions.

He moved back a little from the water's edge once his shorts were wet, content to settle onto the cooling sand. After a moment of peace, a scent reached him that perked up his wolf. His claws descended before he could control himself, his teeth right behind them.

What was that scent?

He sat forward, lifting his nose to trace it. The wind and spray from the ocean slightly interfered and it was pissing him off. But before he could stand, his ears caught the rhythmic footfalls of someone jogging. Squinting into the darkening day, he spotted her headed toward him.

Jesus, she was a work of art. Her tall, curvy body was on display in the shorts and sports bra she jogged in. Her dark caramel skin glistened, catching the light. A gasp of surprise escaped him as he reached her face. His wolf froze within him, pulling back his power. Both man and beast stilled as surprise and old grief rushed to the forefront. He recognized her.

No longer the gangly teenager she'd been, Keisha Calhoun had grown into a stunning woman. The closer she got to him, the more he could feel the strength of her own wolf. She had the type of power that, in his old life, would've had her standing at his side. Even though he was getting out the game, he recognized the perfect blend of strength and beauty that would be an asset to anyone.

Her father had moved through that space like the king he was, so he imagined his daughter would be no less strong. He stood, unable to remain sitting in her presence. A flash of annoyance crossed her face until she was finally able to recognize him in the gathering dark.

She gasped and stopped running a few feet from him. "Devon?"

He smiled and closed the distance between them. "Baby girl."

She flinched. "No one's called me that since my father," she said softly.

"I'm sorry, Keisha," he told her. "How are you?"

She nodded as though that was an answer. There was a tense moment of silence between them as they both took each other in. "I have to go." She moved around him.

He was so stunned by her presence, he didn't even think to stop her. "I want to see you," he called out to her as she retreated.

She looked back but said nothing. He saw the fear in her eyes along with the recognition from her wolf. She was afraid of what they were to each other. He couldn't blame her. She knew nothing about him after ten years apart. How had he missed the fact that they were mates before he went to jail? Her father had been careful to keep her and her mother away from his lifestyle, but still, he'd interacted with her more than once. Only thing he could think was that his wolf hadn't been ready? Hell, she was a teenager the last time he saw her; he wouldn't have thought of her that way either way.

Now, though, she was an adult. A beautiful one at that. He smiled to himself, anticipation and excitement filling him. Mere hours out of prison and a mate nearly fell into his lap. How fortuitous.

Keisha stepped out of the spa-sized shower of her suite and wrapped a fluffy towel around her body, cinching it at her breasts. Her nerves were frayed and the shower hadn't helped one bit. She leaned against the counter, her heart still racing — and it had nothing to do with the three miles she just ran.

Devon was out of prison.

When had he gotten out? She didn't know a lot about him, just the small glimpses of him she'd gotten when he'd come to do her father's bidding. But those glimpses…

Her stomach flipped, her wolf swiping her in agitation. He looked so different now. Gone was the lean, lithe body he'd had the last time she saw him. He was bigger, though not by much, his muscular build just right for her taste. His hair was longer now, locs falling down around his face to his chin. He'd always been so clean-cut around her father.

A full beard covered his face; it went well with his dark, bushy brows and thin mustache. From his Nubian nose down to those full lips that were dark from all the smoking he'd done, Keisha found him attractive. Flawless, even.

The hair on her arms raised before she was able to push the wolf down. She was trying to reconcile what her eighteen-year-old heart had told her about Devon Edwards ten years ago.

Keisha blamed herself for the exacting traits she'd been looking for in a man, but if she were honest with herself, it was her animal that prevented her from settling into a relationship. Her wolf would only settle for one male, and so long as he roamed the Earth, there would never be another for her.

Devon was four years older than her, so he hadn't been checking for her at the time. Besides, her mother had been so adamant about keeping her father's street life separate from them that they'd barely interacted outside of simple hellos. Would he have even noticed her in those times?

Since he worked for her father, Leland would likely not have allowed it anyway. Realizing that Devon was her mate had been a shock and not exactly welcomed. Keisha had been about to graduate high school and had had big plans for herself that included leaving all of Eastfield behind. No way could she live in the shadow of what her father had been, and she definitely hadn't wanted to live the lifestyle her mother had.

In the end, she was happy that she'd kept the news about her mating to herself because her last year of high school had been so chaotic, and none of it had to do with academia. Devon ended up getting arrested, then her father was murdered weeks after his sentencing. A lot of rumors had circulated that the men had been set up, but nothing had come of that. Her wolf had been inconsolable that she'd lost two people so important in her life, and Keisha had grieved heavily for them both. And now, Devon was back.

What was she supposed to do?

How did she feel?

A part of her wanted to run back out the door and track him down. That was purely the wolf talking. If she wasn't careful, the damned animal would have her chasing him across town. But the woman? She was terrified that all she'd run from was coming back to haunt her. Devon represented everything Leland was, and she'd promised herself that she would never get caught up in that. Nothing about being the mate of a hustler appealed to her. Not the easy money, the nights of uncertainty, the insecurity...none of it.

Fuck.

She wanted to call her mother. She needed...she needed to talk to someone.

She cinched her towel tighter and rushed to her phone in the bedroom, dialing the only other person who would understand the turmoil in her life. Her cousin answered on the first ring.

"Are you calling me from the spa, fancy lady?" Lucky teased.

A small smile tilted Keisha's lips. "You'll never believe who I just saw."

The call dropped as her cousin switched to video calling. Keisha rolled her eyes and answered. Lucky was still in her uniform, the striped shirt with the postal services patch on the front. It looked like she was just getting home. Keisha could see her cousin's apartment behind her as she moved through it.

"I can hear something in your voice. What's going on?" Lucky's eyes searched her face.

Her cousin's cocoa skin was smooth and unblemished, her makeup flawless though she'd probably spent hours in the hot mail truck. Her full lips were painted a sedate rose color, her feline-shaped eyes accentuated by cat eye makeup.

"Bitch," Keisha said softly. "I just saw Devon Edwards."

Lucky's eyes widened as she let out a squeal. "Are you serious? How does he look? When did he get out? Oh my God, Keish, what are you going to do?"

Keisha dropped down onto the bed. "Shit, I called you to see if you had any answers."

Lucky's smile dropped. "How do you feel about it?"

She shook her head, praying the tears clogging her throat didn't fall.

"He reminds you of Uncle Leland?" Lucky sighed. "I'm sorry, KeKe."

"But my wolf wants him," she whispered.

Lucky nodded. "And you deserve to have your mate," her cousin said emphatically.

"What if he's still in that lifestyle?" She didn't know that she could go through what Patrice went through.

"You probably aren't going to want to hear this, but I wouldn't be your favorite cousin if I didn't tell you. You are not Auntie. You're stronger than her by far. Whatever you have with Devon would be different based on that fact alone. Finding your mate is special, and you would be foolish to let it slip through your fingers before you even have a full conversation with that man. Remember what happened because you didn't talk to him."

She nodded, cursing the tear that slid down her cheek. She'd chickened out of approaching him and he'd been arrested days later. She knew it wasn't her fault, but for years, she would wonder if her speaking out would've made a difference. Maybe he wouldn't have been where he was when he was arrested. But that didn't mean anything because even if he avoided jail that time, there would've been another.

Or heaven forbid he died with her father the night Leland had been killed. She shivered at the thought.

"You don't have to decide anything right this second. Hell, he just got out of prison. Give him time to get acclimated…and tested." Lucky broke into her thoughts.

Keisha snorted, and Lucky laughed.

"Does he know he's your mate?"

She shrugged. "We didn't talk that long. I was jogging."

Lucky scoffed. "Then the answer is yes. I do wonder if he knew before."

She shook her head. "You know how mama was. Dad's life outside of us had to be out of sight and out of mind."

"Hey, Auntie Pat had to do what she had to do. You can't blame her for that," Lucky reminded her.

"You're absolutely right."

"Okay. So then, it's safe to say he knows and will most definitely be coming after you."

Keisha shuddered as a sudden heated need filled her. He would come after her. Everything she knew about him said he would.

"What do I do?"

"Let that man pursue you. Then let him catch you and knock some of the cobwebs off that coochie."

Keisha choked out a laugh. "Bitch." She chuckled and wiped her face, taking in Lucky's advice.

"KeKe, you 'bout to be mated. To a boss, no less," Lucky said excitedly.

She rolled her eyes. "Girl, he been locked up for ten years. He ain't a boss of shit."

Lucky shook her head. "Don't make no sense that I know more about what's going on on the West side than you do."

"I don't be in the hood like that," she argued with her cousin.

It was a conversation they had often. Keisha's mother was a panther, and so her side of the family — which included Lucky — lived on the south side of town. Her cousin, though, spent a lot of time with Keisha on the west side, much to her aunt's chagrin.

"Your loss," Lucky said, licking her tongue and hitting a quick twerk. "Goodbye, girl."

Lucky stopped dancing. "But seriously, cousin, take it a day at a time. You borrowing trouble before it even shows up."

Keisha nodded. "You're right."

"Of course, I am. Now, it's Saturday night. I'm finna shower and get dressed to meet you at the fancy bar in that hotel and find me a baller."

Keisha laughed. It didn't sound like a bad idea at all. "Pack a bag because I already know you 'bout to drink too much."

"And is!" Lucky told her, winking.

Keisha hung up the phone and took a deep, cleansing breath. Lucky was right. She would take it one day at a time.

5...

Devon settled into the leather seat of the Range Rover, smiling in pleasure. He wondered how long it would take him to get used to this new luxurious lifestyle. Even though he'd made money working for Leland, it was different. This money didn't require constant vigilance to keep. There was no looking over his shoulder, waiting for someone to take what he had. It didn't stop his gaze from pinging around as he drove through town.

He drove through streets he'd been hanging out on in his youth. A lot had changed. There were obvious marks of progress in the newer buildings, though some of the older ones were still nestled in between. Crossing over from the West side to the South side, Devon noticed the difference there as well.

One thing hadn't changed, he noted as he approached the familiar Green Ridge neighborhood. D boys still hugged the corners, and he smiled, knowing no matter who ran the city, that would never change.

He pulled up to the boxing gym where he'd spent a lot of his time as a teenager. His brother was leaning against his Porsche on the phone. The guard Declan kept with him gave him privacy but was not too far away. His brother hung up the phone as Devon hopped out of his car and walked up, slapping hands and pulling him into a hug.

"You ready for this?"

"We'll see," Declan answered.

As they walked in, the place was dark except a light over the table where his friends sat. He smiled at Mason and Jules. Dallas and Julian

Senior stood to the side of them in conversation. A wash of memories overcame him as he looked around the gym. Two boxing rings took up the middle of the large space. Around the rings, along the perimeter of the room, various equipment lined the walls. It was the same as when he'd first arrived as an angry teenager, causing havoc at Winnie's group home where he and his brother had landed.

Dallas Knight had brought him to this same gym to give him an outlet for all that anger. Devon and Silas had gone many rounds in those boxing rings. It was one of the places where he'd forged his friendship with them all. Silas, Julian, Rocco, and he had hit the streets running after they cliqued up. Dallas and Julian Senior had done their best to keep them out of trouble, but four teenagers with an unchecked sense of power had been hell.

Devon's reputation had been well-earned by the time he met Leland. The older wolf had taken him under his wing and guided him through the drug trade. Devon fell for the easy money. In his mind, he was making a way for him and his brother. His friends hadn't judged him even though their own paths had diverged from his. They stayed tight through it all, and Devon didn't know what he would've done without them in his life.

For a moment, he paused just to relish the moment of freedom. His friends were all dressed casually. Mason and Julian both were in sweatsuits and sneakers, looking like they could be ready at a moment's notice if something went down. Mr. D and Senior wore jeans and hoodies, the elder males the epitome of power even at their age. Their casualness underlined the close relationship they all had with each other. There was no barrier of respectability between them. They were all cool, and it was like family when they linked up, even after all these years. It warmed his heart.

"What it do, playboy?" Jules stood and dapped him up in greeting.

He pulled his friend in and slapped his back. Mason was next with his greeting.

"Silas and Rock meeting us here when we done with this shit. With his job, Silas can't be caught up in this," Mason told him as he pulled back from their hug.

Devon nodded his understanding, going over to the older males. "Mr. D."

Dallas smiled at him and gripped his shoulders. "Devon. It's good to see you on this side of the glass."

The eldest Knight had visited Devon many times while he was up the road, and he appreciated it. It had kept him motivated and let him know that Dallas was a man of his word.

"Senior," Devon greeted.

"We staying out of trouble this time, youngin?"

Devon's smile matched Senior's. The two of them understood each other, their wildness matching in every way. It was probably one of the reasons Senior had never judged Devon's decisions, only shaking his head and getting him out of trouble where he'd been able. This last time, though, it for sure had to be a setup because even with the pull these two men had, they couldn't keep him out of the pen.

"This ain't trouble to you?" Devon asked him.

Senior chuckled. "Shit, this light work."

They all sat down and he schooled his features, ready to get to the real reason they were meeting under the cover of darkness.

"Explain it all to me," Devon said, looking at Dallas.

Dallas settled into his chair and kept his gaze. "Cyrus is getting beside himself, first of all. Some of the wolves are coming to me about how the West side is run. I can't intervene without it being war. Not that I'm opposed, but my mate wants me to get somewhere and sit down now that we have grandchildren."

Mason snorted.

"What will it take from me?" Declan asked.

"The best way to do it will be to challenge him where there are witnesses," Dallas told them. "Knowing how he moves, he'll still try and come for you, so both of you will need to be on the lookout."

Devon growled in irritation. He took his job of keeping his brother safe very seriously. Most of the resources and contacts he'd had outside of prison had gone to that the whole time he was locked up. There was no way he would get out and not do the same. Dallas went over the ins and outs of the Motsi while Devon listened carefully. He would take every advantage he could. When Declan had told him about the idea, he'd had some people research the Motsi and its inner workings.

He hadn't been able to get much because the society was insular and very leery of outsiders. It hadn't stopped him from being able to get information on the members of the tri-council, though. He'd collected information about both Cyrus and Micah, wanting to know the inner workings of their hierarchies. From what he'd learned about Micah Crespo, he knew the bear shifter wouldn't interfere with anything wolf-related, so he'd put that information aside to focus solely on Cyrus and his hierarchy, looking for weak points to exploit. He had a couple of ideas, but the information Dallas was giving them would help.

Declan needed to know who in the hierarchy would oppose a challenge to Cyrus, and with that information, they could coordinate their moves. Though he knew the whole thing was dangerous, Devon couldn't help but get excited.

Not long after they finished talking, the doors to the gym opened and in swaggered Silas and Rocco.

Silas held up brown bags in his hand. "It's time to turn up!"

"That's my cue to leave." Dallas laughed, standing. He nuzzled his eldest son's cheeks and headed to the door. "Lock up when y'all done!" he called over his shoulder with Senior on his heels.

"Y'all ain't bring no hoes," Declan commented.

Mason sucked his teeth. "You're welcome to leave, youngin."

Declan growled. "We the same age, bitch."

The table busted out laughing. Drinks were passed out, blunts were lit, and hours later, they were deep into a spades game as the friends caught up with each other. Devon closed his eyes and let the ebb and flow of conversation pass over him. He'd missed so much while he was locked up.

"Yo, you wildin'!" Rocco laughed, shaking his head at Silas. "A few days off got you forgetting you still gotta go home to your busy-body kids."

Devon opened his eyes at the laughter, though with the amount of weed he'd smoked, his lids were still low as fuck. Silas set the bottle on the table and grimaced.

"I knew we'd been going too hard when even Keisha didn't argue about the days off," Silas said.

Hearing Keisha's name had his animal up and interested. All through his time in prison, he'd kept tabs on her and her mother, making sure they were taken care of. It was the least he could do to honor his mentor. He'd felt like it was his duty after Leland was dead, but Ms. Patrice had wanted to cut all ties with the street shit. She had refused his help on multiple occasions. He'd done what he could without intruding, hoping she wouldn't find out.

"Liss didn't even want to let my ass out the house," Rocco grumbled.

"Keisha be working y'all ass to death over there," Mason cracked.

Silas cackled. "I'm supposed to be the boss, but shit, she be on my ass."

Devon growled, and they all turned their attention to him. His wolf rumbled his chest, and Declan sighed.

"Ah, hell nah," his brother fussed.

"You ain't even been in fresh air a whole day, man," Jules said, amused.

"That shit don't matter," he said lowly. "That's me."

"Good luck fitting into her schedule," Rocco teased.

"You ain't lying," Silas said, knocking back another shot. "That girl hustle like nobody I know."

"What does she do for you?" Devon asked out of curiosity. "I thought she was just your assistant."

"That's how it started, but hell, it's been six years. She runs my damn office, and the way she knows how to maneuver politicians and get information..." Silas shook his head. "I give a lot of credit to my team but having her on that team is a big part of it. She knows these systems like the back of her hands."

His chest tightened with pride. He fucking knew she would be good at whatever she did. He nodded his head.

"I thought you were full of shit when you asked me to give her an interview, but I haven't regretted hiring her," Silas told him.

"You didn't tell her I got her that interview, did you?" he asked, suddenly worried for how she would react to that.

"Man, no. Because I wasn't going to hire her on just your word. She earned her spot and then some," his friend assured him.

Devon sat back in his chair, relieved. If Keisha was anything like her mother, she would hate that he'd been helping her from the inside.

"When you even had time to run into that girl, anyways?" Declan asked.

"I saw her on the beach by the house. We didn't have time to exchange information, though." He slid that last sentence in, his focus on Silas.

Rocco snorted, and Silas sighed.

"Aye, man, don't get me cussed out by Keisha," he grumbled before pulling out his phone and sending Devon her number.

He smiled smugly. She could run, but he would chase his mate down. They went back to chilling and kicking it until close to dawn, when his brother insisted that he ride home with him. Jules promised that he would make sure his car got back to him.

6...

Keisha cursed as she swiped her badge. She was late, and she hated being late. It threw her whole day off. She would've made it in fine had she not taken a call from her mother this morning. Patrice needed some work done at the house and wanted to know if her daughter had time to double-check the contractor she'd hired. It had taken Keisha fifteen minutes' worth of internet searching to find out the man had bad reviews all over town.

It wasn't like her mother was helpless, but Patrice saw the good in everyone and gave too many people second chances. The woman was the weirdest mix of street smart and naïve. Patrice was too trusting and sweet, and it was frustrating to say the least. She'd promised her mother that she would find her another contractor, adding yet another thing to do on her list.

And if that wasn't bad, Patrice had let it slip that she'd run into Benny, and her cousin had threatened her mom. Keisha was going to hunt that bastard down the minute she got off work.

"I'm so sorry," she muttered as she walked into Silas's office. "Let me drop this stuff down and I'll get you ready for the conference call you have in ten minutes."

"It's fine, Keisha." He waved off her concern.

She nodded and rushed to her small office next to Silas's, dropping her stuff on top of her desk. Grabbing her tablet and the folder with the itinerary for the upcoming meeting, she rushed back to Silas's office. She was happy that she'd done most of the prep work for the call last night, even if it was technically the last day of her vacation. Silas was watching her when she entered.

"What's wrong?" She paused at the door.

She glanced at Rocco, who was sitting on the sofa off to the side, his laptop open in front of him on the coffee table. He went everywhere with her boss as his main security. The bear didn't even glance up as she came in.

"With me? Nothing. What's up with you?" Silas asked.

Keisha rolled her eyes and went to sit in the chair in front of his desk. His office was large, the recessed lighting creating the illusion of sunshine since their offices were all underground. Silas's desk was simple, wood and metal mixing to look modern. It was clean, holding just his laptop and whatever files he was currently looking through.

Adjusting her tablet, Keisha finally answered him. "Dealing with Patrice."

He smiled. "What does she need?"

"She wants a gazebo in the backyard and called contractors all willy-nilly until she found a thief with complaints a mile long."

Silas snickered. "I know someone who will help. I'll call and get them to send someone."

"You don't have to do that, Silas," she rushed to assure him.

"It's okay to accept help from people, Keisha," he chastised.

She sighed. He was right. "Fine, thank you."

"Of course. Now, settle yourself, you look all frazzled."

Keisha looked down at the simple black slacks and matching blouse, knowing it was not her usual wear and gave away her mood more than anything. She loved bold colors and prints, and most of her clothes reflected that. Even her hair was pulled back into a hasty bun since talking to her mother had taken the time she would usually use to straighten her hair.

She shook her shoulders and took deep breaths. She wished Patrice was the only reason for her unsettled spirit. She'd barely slept since she'd been back from her weekend off. Her wolf was whining, and she couldn't get Devon out of her mind. One part of her wished she'd stopped and let her animal take over the situation, but she already had too much on her plate. Juggling a man — a mate — on top of that was not...

She sighed and shook her head. She'd fucked up. She should've stopped. But she'd let her fear talk her out of it.

An hour later, Keisha hid her yawn as Silas wrapped his call. He eyed her knowingly, smirking as he hung up the phone. She stood and gathered her tablet.

"I'll email over the notes here once I clean them up," she promised him as she headed for the door.

"Keisha," he called to pause her. "I'm leaving after my lunch meeting today. We have an appointment with Carter."

She turned to face him, nodding and opening his schedule to make the adjustments.

"Feel free to do the same."

She was grateful, even though she knew she wouldn't leave directly after lunch. But she could do a lot of her work from home, so she would wrap early. That gave her plenty of time to hunt down her cousin. Afterward, a visit to her mother was in order. Patrice got unruly when Keisha didn't show her face, as evidenced by her hiring a sketchy contractor.

"Also, you know Devon, right?"

That brought her head up and her eyebrows down in confusion. Where was he going with this? She eyed her boss warily, not answering.

Silas hummed and smiled. "You ran into him on the beach sometime this past weekend, I guess."

She nodded reluctantly. A part of her wanted to keep thoughts of Devon to herself.

"He told me to pass on the message that he would see you soon."

A small gasp left her lips as her eyes widened.

Silas chuckled. "It's like that, then. I gave him your number."

"I don't have time for that," she said automatically, though inside she yearned to see him again.

"Fate comes for us all, Keisha," Rocco warned her with a warm smile.

She nodded at them both and escaped the room. Even though her office was next door, her heart was thumping as though she'd run a mile. Closing the door to give herself a small respite, Keisha gathered her restless wolf, taking deep breaths. Anticipation thrummed through her blood, heightening her instincts as though her animal knew something she didn't.

Devon had her number. Would he use it? What would she say if he did call? She'd told Silas she didn't have time for a relationship, and while that was true, it didn't stop the longing. If she were smart, she would take the chance she'd missed when she was a teenager. Devon was out of prison, and maybe hopefully out of the street life. What was stopping her from exploring a mating with him?

Well, for one, she couldn't be sure he was fully out of the streets. She chewed her bottom lip and made a decision. She could kill two birds with one stone. She would find her cousin, who was likely on the corner somewhere 'across the tracks' as they called the West side neighborhood that housed a lot of wolf shifters. It was across the literal train tracks that separated their side of town from downtown Eastfield.

If she went over there — which she very rarely did — then likely, she could get gossip from any number of the cousins she had on her father's side. They always knew what was happening in that neighborhood. Devon Edwards had been a big deal before he'd been locked up. Anyone over there would have some inkling of what he was into now that he was out.

Decision made, she rounded her desk and sat in the chair, hurrying to wrap up her work so she could leave at the same time as her boss.

Devon stepped out of the '72 Charger that Rocco had dropped off at his house last night. It had been a welcome home gift from his friend. The restored car was beautiful, forest green with gold eighteen-inch rims on the tires. The tint was dark, the paint on it gleaming in the sun. He couldn't help but smile as he slid out of the butter-soft seat. His boy had hooked it up. He glanced around the neighborhood, his eyes taking in the decrepit houses and unkempt lawns. Not much had changed across the tracks, including the faces eyeing him from their porches.

A lot of homeowners were a lot older than when he'd last seen them, but their steely-eyed stares were still as sharp. He nodded to some of the old heads, sauntering to the house of his old acquaintance. Terrance met him on the porch, smiling widely.

"Dev walking the streets again!" his friend called out, holding out his hand.

Devon slapped his hand and pulled him in. "And T-Baby still hanging at the trap."

Terrance laughed. "Shit, somebody gotta keep this place running."

"Drew put you in charge?" Devon asked, settling into the worn chair against the wall of the house.

Terrance nodded. "This one and the one over on Twentieth."

"Oh, yeah?"

Devon knew he would eventually need to catch up with Drew to get acquainted with the ins and outs of the way he ran the operation. Even though he was working to get out, he was still curious as to how his friend had been handling things on the outside.

"I been trying to get in touch with him."

"He on the other side of the state on a run," Terrance told him.

Devon frowned. "Why he doing the runs?"

"Claim he can't trust nobody," Terrance answered with a shake of his head. "You back now, so you can tighten this shit up the way you had it before you got knocked."

He shook his head. "I ain't on that. That's why I'm trying to get up with Drew."

Terrance eyed him with surprise. "You tired of going in and out, huh?"

They both laughed. Devon's wolf perked up, his hand immediately going to his waist when he spotted a car flying into the neighborhood.

The small sedan parked across the street, and to his surprise, his mate stormed out of the car, rushing to the front door of the house. If memory served him, Leland's sister lived there. She banged on the door until a male stepped out. The two of them started yelling at each other.

Terrance cursed. "God almighty, man. Here they go."

"What's going on?" Devon asked, his eyes not leaving his mate.

"Keisha and Benny stay getting into it. She don't come out this way that much, but when she does, it's because Benny done got her mama caught up in some shit. You know how sweet Ms. Patrice is. She be trying to help that knucklehead."

Devon stood up, ready to intervene. "Lord, this girl finna have me out here wildin' already."

"That's you?" Terrance asked in surprise.

Devon nodded, wanting everyone on this side of town to know that and know she was off-limits.

"You better go get her, then, because Benny got a hands problem when it comes to women," Terrance said casually.

Devon cursed and headed across the street. Of course, his wolf wouldn't pick someone easy. Shit, he wasn't an easy person to deal with, so why he thought he would get a mate who couldn't handle that was a delusion all on its own. He jogged across the street just in time for Keisha to cock back and punch her cousin. It wasn't no small punch either — there was power behind it because Benny rocked back.

He growled as Benny's incisors dropped and he lifted his hand. Devon caught him and squeezed his wrist.

"I wish the fuck you would," he growled lowly.

Keisha stepped back with a gasp of surprise as Devon squeezed tighter. She punched her cousin once more, this time in the stomach. Lord have mercy. Devon could only shake his head. Partly in pride because clearly, his mate was with the shits, but the other part was aggravation because what had been Keisha's end goal here?

He was curious to know how she saw this whole situation playing out had he not been around to stop her cousin from striking her back. Or did she even care? She lowkey looked like she could scrap either way. He added *impulsive* to the list of her traits he was starting in his head.

Benny yelled out as Devon squeezed his hand tighter at just the thought of touching his mate. He released her cousin after he heard a crack, a rumble of satisfaction rattling his chest as her cousin cradled a hand that he knew was broken. If the male was lucky, it would heal in a few hours.

Emboldened by his help, Keisha stepped closer to Devon's back. "Threaten Patrice Calhoun one more time and I got something for your ass."

There was pain in Benny's eyes, his wolf flashing in his gaze. "Ain't nobody threaten yo' fucking mama, KeKe," he outright lied.

"Don't call her phone, and definitely don't get your mama to call her either when you get your goofy ass into some more shit."

"Fuck both of y'all!" Benny snapped.

"Aye!" Devon barked out. He stepped closer, allowing his claws to lower.

People from the neighborhood were gathering, drawn to the drama. Devon wanted to hurt the male, but he couldn't be sure what the neighbors would do. They weren't likely to call the police, but all the same, he took in a calming breath.

"Watch how you talk to that one," Devon warned him.

Fear finally leaped into her cousin's eyes, and he stepped back, but it was quickly overridden by anger. "Devon, this shit a family matter."

"Well, that's my family, and she said what the fuck she said. Pass that fucking message on to whoever you need to."

Benny swallowed, and after a tense stare-off, he nodded.

Devon stepped back, never taking his eyes off him. "Back in the car, love."

He expected her to argue; he could feel the heat of her anger on his back. But surprisingly, she didn't. He turned his back to Benny, knowing the other male would take it for the disrespect it was. Hell, he wanted the male to jump — it would give him a reason to beat his ass. He walked his mate to her car and helped her in.

"I don't need any further help," she said. The whole tone of her voice had changed, the roughness she used with her cousin smoothed out. "Thank you, though, for what you did," she said somewhat reluctantly.

He smiled and leaned over the driver's side. His eyes skimmed her face, and he saw the residual aggravation there along with the wolf she was trying to bury. Her hair was coming undone from the bun at the back of her head, surrounding her face in a halo of textured curls. It made her look vulnerable and so beautiful. He swallowed the words he'd intended for her, instead cupping her chin gently.

"I was going to tell you that you can't be punching people and not expecting them to react, but don't even worry about it. I got your back now, so you can slap people up and down these streets if you need to."

A ghost of a smile skimmed her lips. "He's my dad's peoples and…" She shook her head and sighed. "Never mind. Can I close my door now?"

"Give me your number."

She rolled her eyes.

"Aht-aht," he said softly.

"You already got my number from my boss. Which, how do the two of you even know each other?" She looked around the neighborhood.

"You looking like your boss don't know corner boys."

"You get out of prison to be a corner boy again?" Her expression had dropped, and he felt that he'd lowered in her estimation. His wolf didn't like that at all, whining.

"I did not. But that's beside the point."

She shrugged, but her expression cleared, relief crossing her face before she covered it. "You right. Silas knows all kinds of people."

She dismissed him, pulling her chin from his hand. Her resistance gave him pause, and his wolf rumbled his chest. He could already see shawty was finna be a handful.

"You've grown into a beautiful woman," he told her. She nodded her thanks. He leaned forward and nuzzled the side of her cheek. "Get from this side of the tracks," Devon ordered before stepping back. "I'ma call you. I expect you to answer."

Her eyes flashed for a moment before she tamped it down. "You look like a menace, and I'm not trying to get my feelings hurt or be fighting bitches up and down these streets."

Devon kissed her forehead and stepped back, not trying to hear all that. He allowed her to fully get into the car. She slammed her door and he chuckled, tapping the top and stepping away so she could pull off. Keisha eyed him one last time before starting her car and doing just that.

This would be fun. He knew he had that shit with his brother to worry about, but chasing his mate sounded like just the thing to do to offset that stress. He smiled and eyed Benny, who quickly rushed into his mother's house. Something told him he would have to deal with that motherfucker, but he needed to feel his mate out before he went around taking people out behind her. He answered the phone ringing in his pocket. It was Silas.

"Yeah?"

"Your new mother-in-law needs a gazebo in her backyard."

"Now, how you know that?" he asked. He didn't know shit about building shit, but he knew some people he could call.

"Because Keisha came in the office stressed about it."

He nodded, though he knew his friend couldn't see it. "Good looking out."

"Good luck." Silas chuckled and hung up.

Devon sighed because he wasn't quite ready to see Ms. Patrice and open that box of grief. But Silas had said it was stressing his mate, and that he wouldn't allow.

7 . . .

Devon took a deep breath and stared at the house in front of him. It had taken him a couple of days after talking to Silas to finally work up the nerve to come by. This house was the last known location he had for Patrice Calhoun, and everything looked the same, telling him the woman was still in residence. The dark blue exterior was new, but the desert landscaping full of various cacti and white stones was the same. Snake plants lined the concrete walkway to the front door and gave the whole yard an elegant look. For a moment, memories from his youth came back and hit him hard.

Leland Calhoun had taken a young Devon, straight out of county jail, under his wing. For years, the man had groomed him in the ins and outs of the drug game, teaching all that he'd known. Leland was big on the West side, the only dealer actually connected to the plug. It kept him above all the others who had to scavenge for their supply.

At the time, Devon thought it the only way to feed himself and keep his little brother on the straight and narrow. His first brush with jail had him wanting to go straight, but he'd seen so much potential in Declan, and he would've done whatever it took to keep his brother in school and out of the streets. He chuckled to himself because even with that, Declan had found himself on the other side of the law.

Devon had worked for Leland for a lot of years before the older male turned everything he knew over to him. He'd gotten sent up the road within a year of that exchange, his mentor killed right after. Everything about it had screamed setup, but he'd spent the first few months in prison mourning. Finding out who'd set him up hadn't been a priority. Now that he was out, though, and about to be in the lives of the family Leland had left behind... The questions he'd pushed aside were pushing themselves forward.

Shaking away his thoughts, he observed the neighborhood. Leland had set his mate and daughter up in a nice house on the edge of the neutral zone and wolf territory. He'd kept them on the West side but far enough away from the shit Leland had done in the streets, hoping it would keep them safe. It had worked, as far as Devon knew.

His wolf bristled at all the scent markers across the neighborhood. The markers were triggering. It had always given him a sense of insecurity that he'd had nothing to mark as his own. Even as he'd earned his own money and bought his own place, that insecurity hadn't left. He'd hated it when he was in prison too. His animal liked its space and the encroaching scents tended to feel oppressive.

He got out of the car. Wasting time stalling would get him nowhere. He knocked on the door and waited, tension tightening his shoulders. Patrice answered the door, her face confused until she got a good look at him. The confusion cleared as a wide smile took over her beautiful face.

"Devon Edwards," she said softly, pulling him into her arms.

He closed his eyes as her warmth covered him. "Hi, Ms. Patrice." He cleared the gruffness from his throat.

The strength of Ms. Patrice's panther was palpable and had always been. She'd always been sweet to the hustlers in her husband's orbit, but everyone had known not to fuck with her, and that had nothing to do with Leland's name and everything to do with how powerful her animal was. Leland had always said that Patrice's delicate outer appearance hid a core of steel.

"Come in, come in." She guided him into the house.

Keisha was tall like her father, but Patrice barely came to Devon's chest. Her trim body was hidden under the flowing dress she wore, her bare feet silent on the tile floors.

The soothing energy of her home sank into him. He'd been to this house only a few times and maybe twice when he'd taken over for Leland, and everything about it was changed now. The décor was different, more feminine…softer. He exhaled and a weight he'd carried into her space shed. He was having a hard time adjusting to all of his new circumstances, but none of that mattered in the home this woman had lovingly curated.

"You want something to drink?"

"I'll take coffee if you have it," he murmured. Hell, he needed it. Even after a week out, sleep was elusive for him.

She smiled and beckoned him into the kitchen. He took a seat at the counter and watched as she prepared the coffee machine. Devon glanced around the kitchen and noted little small things that could be done to update the house. Now that he knew what Keisha was to him, taking care of the two women was on his list of priorities.

"You look like a completely different person," Patrice commented. "The last time I saw you, you were a cocky young man, ready to take on the world."

He chuckled softly. "Not much has changed in that aspect. Though my plans don't include running up and down these streets."

She gave him a relieved smile. "Well, thank God for that."

"I'm sorry about Leland, Ms. Patrice." He'd always regretted not being out and able to watch his mentor's back.

She waved her hand. "Leland always knew the inevitable ending to his lifestyle."

Almost ten years had passed since her mate's death and he could feel her grief, so he nodded his understanding.

"Thank you for what you've been doing," she said softly.

He sat up straighter in surprise. "You knew?"

Patrice scoffed. "I turned down the money, but you didn't think I would notice the security? Some of the boys still come through here and check on me."

He nodded because it was what they should've been doing. Leland had had an impact on them all. It was the least they could've done.

"It wasn't your job to take care of us," she told Devon sternly. "Leland left us comfortable, and I didn't feel right taking money from you."

He disagreed, and without rehashing old arguments, he simply told her, "It was my job then, and even more so now."

Patrice tilted her head and studied him. "Why do you say that?"

He changed the subject, not wanting to get into his potential mating with her daughter. At least not until he'd talked to her about it.

"I heard you wanted to do a gazebo in your backyard?"

It was her turn to look surprised. She narrowed her eyes. "Did my daughter tell you that?"

"Not directly," he said.

She stared, and her panther prodded his wolf before she gasped. She quickly turned back to the coffee pot. "You're…" She paused. "So you know she's your mate?"

"You've known this whole time?"

"My daughter and I are close." She poured the hot liquid with shaking hands. "There was a time after Leland… We talked a lot, fighting though our respective grief." She set the pot back and gave him the full weight of her stare and power. "Are you ready for her?"

Devon didn't bother hiding anything from the woman. He wanted them all to be close. It was important to him for their upcoming family unit to be tight.

"There's some stuff I want to handle first, but yes. I don't plan to run from our mating."

Patrice sighed and sat down next to him. "I don't want the same life I lived for my daughter."

"I'm out the game, Ms. Patrice. Just tying up loose ends to help my brother."

She gave a surprised gasp.

"Declan wants the tri-council seat, and in order to be there for him, I need to be out."

"That's its own danger," she warned.

He nodded in understanding. "I'm here, and I don't plan on going anywhere," he assured her.

She grabbed his hand and squeezed. "Keisha's stubborn."

"I assumed, with Leland being her father."

Patrice laughed. "God, she's so much like him. Got the nerve to look and act like him," she said wistfully.

"I'll take care of her. Of you both. I swear."

Her eyes watered. "I keep telling you, I don't need taking care of. I can do that myself."

"I don't doubt it, but out of respect for Leland and now my mate, I got you from here on out. Which brings me to my next question. Benny been giving you problems?"

She scoffed and stood. "That boy got a lot of mouth and almost no heart to back it up."

He chuckled. "Your daughter was 'bout to knock his head off his shoulders."

"Just like her damn daddy," Patrice muttered.

Devon laughed. "Come show me what you want in the back so I can call some people."

He was glad they'd gotten everything out in the open. He was going to pursue Keisha, whether she was ready for it or not, and getting Ms. Patrice on his side was just but one step toward that.

Keisha's knee bounced as she worked at her kitchen counter. She'd changed her second bedroom into a closet, so she used her kitchen as her office when she worked from home. It had been a couple days since she'd last seen Devon, and her wolf was restless, urging her to seek him out. Instead of listening to her animal, she'd done what she always did when she was unsure — buried herself in the minutiae of work. Sipping from her wine glass, she scrolled through the research the office was working through.

Even though she was currently fighting with her wolf about Devon, she was considerably more relaxed since she'd taken those days off. But the animal was getting impatient. Soon, she would need to find him, if only to placate her wolf.

The phone at her elbow rang, and she froze. If it was her mother, she was not apologizing for punching Benny. He deserved to be fully cursed out. His mother had spent nearly her last damn dime to get him out of lockup, only for him to turn around and be on the same corner. The fact that he'd threatened her mother when she saw him still had Keisha hot. She frowned when she noticed it was an unknown number. She answered, and the smooth tones of Devon's voice poured out. Her pulse sped up.

"Hey, mamas."

"Devon," she greeted, twirling her hair around a finger in nervousness.

"What you doing?"

"Working."

"Work day over, baby," he gently chided.

She scoffed. "Not for me. Did you want something in particular, or did you hit my line to bother me?"

He chuckled. "You gon' be mean to me, Key?"

She couldn't help the warmth that spread through her body. "I'm not being mean," she defended.

"How was your day, love?" he asked, ignoring that.

She sighed and closed her laptop, deciding to give in to the pushy animal both inside her and on her phone. "It was fine. Busy, but I like busy days."

"I want to see you again."

She considered what to say. She was just chastising herself for brushing him off earlier. Her wolf had been sulking along with pushing for her to hunt him down. Giving in, she relaxed her shoulders.

"Where?" she said after the silence.

"Last time I saw you, you were eighteen. What does adult Keisha like to do?"

"I like fancy shit. Dinner, theater, all that," she replied, testing him.

"Okay. Give me a date and time."

She sucked in a surprised breath. She'd expected him to scoff at her choices. The last time she'd seen Devon before he was locked up, he was West side down. She couldn't have imagined that had changed in the ten years he'd been in prison. But for her, he was willing to try. She was flattered by that.

"I can make time on Saturday," she said flippantly.

He chuckled, seeing past her ruse. "Okay, then. I'll come get you at six."

Just like that. Another point in his favor. "Six it is."

"So, tell me about yourself," he prodded.

She couldn't help the smile that overtook her face. "Aren't you supposed to save that for the date?"

"I don't think a single conversation will encompass everything there is to know about you," he rebutted.

She smiled, liking his answer. "Well, in that case, where do you want me to start?"

"Anywhere," was his answer.

She grabbed her wine glass and made her way to the sofa. "You know what happened to daddy after you got knocked."

He hummed for her to continue, and she paused, waiting for all the grief filling her to shift away. It still managed to catch her off guard. It had only been nine years, and it felt like they would never get past it some days. She curled onto the sofa, tucking her feet beneath her.

Keisha cleared her throat. "Mama insisted that I go to college anyway. I left the state, though not far. I studied political science. When I finished...I don't know. I missed Eastfield, even though I swore I would leave this place behind. I told mama I wanted to come home and applied for a job in the Motsi. Silas Knight offered to let me interview for him instead, and I hopped on it. I've been doing it ever since."

"You like it?"

"Love it," she told him.

"I fucks with that."

Why the simple sentence felt like support, she didn't know, but it warmed her internally. She wondered if that would change once they started dating. Most men she'd gone out with had admired her drive at first until it started to interfere with the time they thought they should be entitled to. It had made dating annoying, to say the least. She'd given it up for situationships because she'd not been interested in juggling the egos of grown men.

"What do you plan on doing since you're home?"

He sighed. "That's what I'm dealing with now. It's a little overwhelming to be out and my circumstances be so different. My brother is grown and all the reasons I was doing what I was doing are gone. So where does that leave me?"

She pulled a blanket over her body, interested in where his head was at. "So now you have time to think of yourself and less about survival."

He chuckled. "Right. Now I'm asking myself what that even looks like."

Tucking a pillow beneath her head, Keisha settled more into her sofa, fully intrigued with the direction of their conversation.

"Is it just you and your brother?"

"Until there was you."

Keisha shivered at the promise in his voice. "Be serious."

Devon chuckled. "Our father died before Declan was born and then our mother died as he was born."

Her heart went out to them both. "So you've been taking care of him your whole life."

"I was six when mom died. We were sent to live with her mother, then when she died, we were put into the system."

She hummed in sympathy and decided to lighten the subject. "How did you meet my boss?"

He laughed. "Our last group home was on the south side. Mr. D and his wife were in and out, making sure the kids had what they needed. Silas was with the shits. I don't know, me, him and Julian just clicked. Then came along Rock, and it was trouble everywhere we went."

She shook her head. "I can imagine."

The two of them spent the rest of the night talking, which was a surprise to her. She didn't think they would have anything in common outside of knowing her father, but they talked with an ease that made her comfortable. She was smiling wide by the time they'd hung up the phone in the wee hours of the night.

8...

Devon, once again, found himself across the tracks, hanging in front of a known trap house. It was a different neighborhood from the last one, but still in the hood. This time it was for business, and as he sat on the porch, shooting the shit with Terrance, he realized that he was already tired of it. He was in his thirties, and the time for hanging out on the corner was done.

It had everything to do with Keisha. Fate worked funny sometimes. He'd been wondering what to do with his life and fate had dumped his mate squarely into his lap to remind him what was at stake with his newfound freedom.

As he sat waiting on his friend to arrive, he reminded himself that easy money never coincided with an easy lifestyle. He had only to look to Keisha to drive that point home. Her father losing his life to the streets was a stark reminder. He didn't want to abandon his mate the way Leland had done his, although it had been outside of her father's control.

Especially after talking to Ms. Patrice.

Devon didn't want either woman to have to relive that type of lifestyle. Thinking of the two of them removed the stress he felt over making this final decision. Stepping away from the game was but one way he would show both women that he was serious about his mating.

"You for real finna step away?" Terrance asked, taking a deep inhale of the blunt he was smoking.

"I gotta be done with this shit, man. These streets don't give a fuck about us."

Terrance hummed. "And you turning all the connects over to Drew?"

Devon eyed him, wondering if he had a problem with that. All throughout his prison sentence, Drew was the one he'd left in control of everything. There was nothing about his friend to make him think it wasn't the right decision. They'd been friends for as long as Devon could remember. But before he could get clarity on Terrance's question, the man in question pulled up. Terrance left and went inside, leaving him alone with his friend.

Devon checked his watch as Drew stepped out of the Mercedes truck and swaggered over to him. "So we just showing up when we feel like it?"

His voice was teasing, but Drew understood that Devon wasn't joking. His friend winced.

"That's my bad, D. Fucking around with Claudia."

"She still on bullshit?"

Devon was surprised his friend was still messing with the woman, but he kept the words to himself. If his friend wasn't tired after tussling with that cougar for six years, then who was he to say anything?

"I shouldn't have to fight this hard to see my kid, man. I already know what you finna say." Drew held up his hand. "You told me she was on bullshit, but you know how it is. Besides, my son is a wolf, and I can't trust them cougars to raise him the way he should come up. If he was a feline, maybe."

Devon gave his boy grace because he was locked up before the money he'd made could go to his head, so who was to say how he would've been on the outside? He prided himself on his self-control, but he couldn't say what temptation would've wrought in his life.

"You checked out the trap?" Drew asked him after taking a deep breath.

Devon nodded. "Workers moving like they should, money coming in. You been doing what you said you would."

"You like the changes?"

Devon looked down the block and grunted. The neighborhood was quieter than the other; there was normal traffic and hanging out for the type of hood it was, but nothing too out of the way. The corner boys blended in yet were conspicuous enough for buyers to see them. It kept undue attention off the house where they operated. Normally, there would be people hanging around, bringing attention to the place, but outside of Devon and Drew on the porch shooting the shit, wasn't too much to make it stand out. If anyone was observing, it looked like a regular suburban house.

"Walk me through it," he ordered.

Drew took Terrance's spot on the porch and they chopped it up as he explained the changes he'd made and the different traps he had set around the West side. Nearly thirty minutes later, Devon was ready to leave, having a full understanding of the way the money was moving.

He stood and dapped his friend. "Shit looks good. You ready to take over the whole thing?"

Drew's eyes widened. "Wait…you serious?"

"I'm out, Drew. I told you before I left prison. I can't be doing this shit with the moves my brother's trying to make. Plus, I met my mate."

"No shit?" Drew said. "So, Declan is serious about the council seat?"

Devon nodded.

"That's what's up, then."

Devon's wolf rose, the hair on the back of his neck standing up as he automatically reached for his gun. He turned to see what had his wolf upset when he saw a dark car slowing as it approached the house.

"Shit!" he cursed and ducked right as they started firing.

Booming gunfire rained overhead as Drew and Devon hit the dirt, scrambling for cover. Debris exploded all around them, bullets whistling past as the engine of the car roared. Devon tucked himself tight behind the post of the stairs and fired back at the masked shifter hanging from the back window. The rest of the block scattered, and as soon as it started, it was over. Over the gunshots, the sound of squealing tires and yelling was loud. Devon managed to get another shot off as the car sped off and turned a corner.

His heart was racing, his wolf thrashing inside in rage as he finally stood. Adrenaline flushed through his blood, and fur rippled down his back as his animal nearly forced his shift. His breath sawed in and out of his lungs as he fought to calm his body. Barely a week out and he was already in some shit.

A stillness fell over them when it was all done. Dogs barking mixed with car alarms was the only noise as the dust began to settle. Drew and Devon locked eyes to confirm they weren't hit, and both men hopped up, barking orders for men to find out what just happened and who was involved.

"What the fuck?" Devon asked, keeping his gun down at his side, just in case. His wolf paced his body. He needed to get from across the tracks before he ended up breaking his promise to Ms. Patrice.

"Drew, let me know if you find anything out," Devon told his friend as he jogged to his truck.

He inspected it and cursed at the bullet hole in the passenger door. He was glad he'd parked down the street. Declan would kill him if he found out what happened.

"Bet. I'll take care of it. Stay safe."

"Always," Devon said, getting into his truck.

It wasn't until he'd driven out of the neighborhood that his emotions caught up to him. He could've lost his life before he even got a chance to spend any time with his mate. If he wasn't serious about getting out before, he was now.

Keisha kicked her shoes off under her desk and sighed. The smell of lemon pepper wings was calling her name. She should thank Julissa for getting hired because Rocco spoiled his mate, and a lot of times, that meant lunch for the office. She could've been eating in the conference room with the others, but she valued the quiet time of her lunch. It helped her reset before the busy afternoon.

Her office was small, with just enough room for her desk, a chair in front of it, and a couple of bookshelves. The walls were a simple white, but she'd covered them with paintings in shades of green to match the faux plants in the corner. It was her little oasis at work and she loved it, even if she spent most of her time in Silas's office.

She cursed as her phone rang, rolling her eyes when she noticed the caller. It was her cousin Sabrina from her father's side, which meant it was finna be some bullshit. Her brows pulled down in a frown as she realized the number of missed calls and text messages. It had taken her less than ten minutes to fix a plate in the conference room. What in the hell had happened in that time?

Her heart raced as she immediately went to the worst.

"Yeah, Bri?"

She put the call on speaker so that she could go through the messages.

"Girl, Devon was involved in a drive-by shooting," her cousin announced immediately.

Keisha's stomach turned as she read the texts confirming that, though the messages didn't give her any of the pertinent information. Trembles took over her body, the top of her head buzzing with the beginning of panic. Her breath froze in her lungs at Sabrina's announcement.

"No one was hurt," Sabrina said in a huff when Keisha didn't give her a reaction.

Keisha cursed and sat back in her chair, her lids dropping as she blew out the breath she'd held. "Why would you call me at work and tell me that? What the fuck, Bri?"

Her cousin sucked her teeth. "I thought you would want to know. Benny said Devon was going around claiming you. You ain't concerned about your supposed man?"

Keisha ignored the dig. "You just called to see if I had more information than you had. Why? Who you asking for?"

She knew the way Sabrina worked. She and her cousin got along, but the woman liked gossip — and loved even more to be able to say she got her gossip from the source.

Sabrina sighed in irritation. "Girl, that's the last time I try and help you out."

"Save it, Bri. Who is she?"

"You remember Delilah Saunders? She used to mess with Devon before he got sent down the road."

"What she got to do with me?" Keisha asked impatiently. She knew this would happen. Devon was someone that everyone knew. It was only a matter of time before women started coming out of the woodwork.

"Y'all together or not?" Sabrina asked.

"None of her damn business," Keisha snapped.

"So, that's a yes," Sabrina confirmed. "It's family over everything this way, so I'ma nip that right in the bud."

Keisha sighed. "Bri, I ain't trying to start no mess."

"Ain't no mess. That's my friend, but Benny said y'all mates, and you know we don't play that shit," Sabrina assured her.

"I ain't worried about no one who was with Devon prior to me," she told her cousin. "So, if that's all you wanted, I'm hanging up so I can get back to work."

"Do you, bougie girl," Sabrina said, and Keisha chuckled because only her family called her that.

"Thanks, cuz," she said reluctantly, at the end of the day still appreciative that her cousin was looking out for her.

"Always. Tell Auntie it's 'bout time for another kickback," Sabrina said and hung up.

Keisha shook her head. She would not be relaying that message to Patrice because Keisha ended up doing too much work at their family barbecues and she was not in the mood. She drummed her fingers along the top of her desk, her lunch long forgotten.

She wanted to call him and find out what happened but hearing about Delilah had her pissed. She ignored the next few calls that came in, irritated with the fact that she would be fielding calls all day from nosy cousins. She was sure Benny had told everyone about Devon, and now with him involved in a shootout, everyone would be calling to get any information she had on it. Gossip moved through her family at the speed of light. Her wolf whined, needing something to reassure her that Devon was fine. She gave in and dialed him.

"Hey, my baby," he answered the phone quickly.

He sounded fine, no hint of worry in his voice and no sense that anything was wrong. If it wasn't Sabrina that she'd talked to, she would've thought the information filtered back to her was wrong.

"What are you doing?" she tested.

"Making some moves, catching up with people I ain't seen in a minute." His voice wrapped around her and her wolf finally calmed. "I'm looking forward to seeing you tomorrow."

"Oh, yeah? Are there any other women you're looking forward to seeing now that you're out?" She silently cursed because she hadn't meant to bring that up.

He sucked his teeth. "My baby, I'm sure your wolf already told you what it is with us. I have no plans on fucking up our mating fooling with other women."

It soothed her anger and she cleared her throat. "Is everything okay?"

"All is well over here," he said smoothly.

Her irritation spiked and she hmphed. He was going to pretend like the drive-by didn't happen at all? She didn't know how she felt about that. She didn't want to start anything with him keeping shit from her. As Lucky reminded her, she was nothing like Patrice. She couldn't compartmentalize her life like that.

Devon chuckled, clearly sensing her mood. "Say what you gotta say, love."

"I don't have anything to say," she lied. "I'll see you tomorrow."

"Call me when you get home," he ordered.

She sighed in aggravation. "Have you ever thought to ask?"

He just laughed and hung up, giving her her answer.

9...

Devon whistled as he pulled up to the building his brother owned and worked out of. Declan had done well for himself. He parked his car and got out, sliding his gun into the back of his pants. After what happened yesterday, he had no plans to be caught slipping. The Range Rover was at Rock's shop being repaired. His friend hadn't asked any questions about it, just promised to have it back quickly.

He kept his guard up as he sauntered up to the building. Declan had already cursed him out yesterday about the drive-by when he'd called to push their meeting back to today. In the back of his mind, he wondered what they needed to meet about, but he didn't ask any questions. He didn't have any plans until this evening, so he was good with it.

He smiled at the fancy office, stepping into the shiny elevator as the receptionist for the building followed him with her eyes. He nodded his head at her as the doors closed and could only laugh. The old him would've maybe taken her up on her offer, but he was not playing when it came to his mate. Yesterday when she'd asked him what was going on, he knew she'd heard about the drive-by. He'd wanted to tell her the truth, but there was no way he would risk their date tonight. Rocco warned him that Keisha would be a hard one to crack and he wasn't taking any chances.

He strode through his brother's office, spotting his guard, which told him which office Declan occupied. A woman guarding the entrance smiled politely as he stopped in front of her. She didn't look in the least bit intimidated, and Devon wondered what kind of people she saw on the daily.

"Can I help you?"

"I'm here to see my brother." Devon stood next to her desk, not wanting to intrude on her work.

"Of course. Mr. Edwards is expecting you," she told him, standing.

He waved her into her seat. "I can make my way back," he said, headed toward the small hallway between her and the guard looming over Declan's office.

The guard moved to the side and allowed him entrance, and Devon smiled at his brother behind his giant mahogany desk. The office was huge and lavishly appointed. Large windows covered the walls behind Declan, showcasing downtown Eastfield. The plush carpet had his footsteps silent as he walked across it. Pride for his little brother swelled his chest.

"You got that shit on, my boy," he complimented his brother as he stood to greet him.

Declan rounded the desk, and they clasped hands before bumping their foreheads together. "Sit down, man."

Devon sat in the plush leather chair in front of Declan's desk as his brother went back to his seat. "We could've just done lunch if you wanted to see me, little brother."

Declan snorted. "You a man of leisure all of a sudden?"

He'd been chilling hard all week and liked it. He could continue doing that for a while, according to the shit Declan had told him on the plane ride home, but Devon knew that he needed to be active or he would be tempted to get back into the same shit that had gotten him into trouble. Yesterday was a stark reminder of what lay in that direction.

"Just getting my bearings," he said.

"Like I said, ain't no rush." Declan slid a folder across his desk to him.

Devon opened it and frowned at the printouts inside. "What's this?"

"Your portfolio. It lists the profits from the investments I made for you, as well as the profits from the three utility patents I filed on your behalf."

"Wait…" Devon's eyes skimmed over the numbers, a sense of disbelief disorienting him.

He remembered the conversations he'd had with his brother about ideas for improvements he'd wanted to make to some of the machines they worked on in the prison where he'd been housed. He'd started vocational training while he was there to show good behavior, but he'd actually enjoyed learning electronics and HVAC shit. In return for the training, the prisoners had been put to work putting together circuit boards for pennies on the dollar.

It had been too close to slave labor for his peace of mind. Declan had thought the same and told Devon to send him schematics of his ideas instead of passing them along to the company they did work for. He hadn't had a lot of time to tinker, but Devon had used the phone he conducted his illegal business with to research. Instead of smuggling in drugs and other paraphernalia, he'd had books and materials he could use to draw snuck in.

From the numbers on this sheet, the shit had paid off. "You were patenting the shit I sent you?"

Declan nodded. "I had some people out here look it over to double-check your work and then patented them under a company in your name."

"You was really moving for me," Devon said, a lump growing in his throat. "Man, I was supposed to be taking care of you."

"And you did," Declan insisted. "No way I got this shit without you. The money you gave me seeded more than you see here."

"These numbers can't be right." Devon shook his head.

His portfolio was worth fucking *millions*. And not little millions. The money he'd made in the streets would've never touched these numbers. He was stunned as he read the spread of where his brother was investing his money. He'd assumed he owned small businesses all over town, but Declan had gone beyond that. He flipped through to the next page.

"Licensing?"

"It allows some of the big manufacturers of air conditioning units to use your technology without owning it."

"Shit…Dec," he said quietly.

"This is… I'm only showing you this because you been hanging out with old company."

Devon shook his head. "I'm turning all that shit over to Drew. I'm getting out," he promised his brother.

Declan studied him. "I'm not trying to lose you to no bullshit, Dev," he said softly. "Stay from 'cross the tracks, man," he grumbled, reinforcing the lecture he'd given him from yesterday.

"You gon' need an army behind you whether you want to believe it or not, little brother."

Declan sighed.

"If the hood ain't behind you, it don't matter if you sitting in that chair. Cyrus is able to move how he move because he got shooters waiting for people to step out of line. You gotta have the same."

Declan leaned against his desk. "And I guess that's what you're doing?"

"The dope boys need my connects. They can't get to the plug without me. How you think I kept money coming into our pockets until you took off with this?"

Declan nodded and got up to pace behind his chair.

"Leland left all that shit with me, and don't shit move on the west side without that knowledge," he explained.

"So, you not out?"

Devon sighed because that wasn't what he was saying. "I been gone nearly a decade. I just have to make sure the person I pass it over to will use it to feed our people, but also, I need it to buy loyalty to us."

Declan rubbed his chin. "You think it'll work?"

"I been finessing for the two of us since you could walk, my baby. I'll make shit shake."

His brother sighed. "Just be careful, please."

"Shit, I'm on my best behavior. My mate don't play that shit." He chuckled.

"I like her for you," Declan agreed.

He held up the folder. "So, let's say I wanted to spend the rest of my life tinkering in that workshop you built me?"

His brother smiled in relief. "Then I'll do what I've been doing and make it make money for you."

He hummed because in all his life, he would've never envisioned this for himself. But the more he thought about it, the more it appealed to him. His mate worked a lot. Like a fucking lot, and taking care of her was about to be his new favorite thing to do. If he closed his eyes, he could almost picture the life they could have if he got this right. He swallowed the emotion clogging his throat and nodded.

"Bet. But in the meantime, I'ma get you that fucking seat."

"I never doubt you," Declan said, matter-of-fact, settling back into his chair. He slid him a brown envelope. "All the cards and access information to your accounts. There's a credit card in there too, even though I know how you feel about that."

Devon leaned forward and grabbed the envelope, dumping the cards into his hand. He'd look over the other information later. "I need you to get cards made for my baby too. As my mate, she needs access to all this shit."

Declan smiled. "Simping fresh out of prison, huh?"

Devon laughed. "Fuck you, baby brother." He stood, tucking the folder and envelope under his arm. "Let me let you get back to your day, then. I'm gonna spend some of these funds to ball out for my mate on our first date."

His brother chuckled and shook his head. "Good luck with that, baby."

He saluted Declan and left his office in a good ass mood. Certainly better than when he'd arrived. What could he buy for his mate that would make her day easier?

Devon squinted at the modern apartment building as he pulled up. It was in the nicer part of the West side, one of the areas that had been heavily gentrified. Spotting Keisha's sedan, he pulled in next to it.

A frown bunched his brows as he realized she was on the ground floor of the building. Nah, that wouldn't fly. There was a chance that she wouldn't be ready to move in with him, but he needed to talk to her about something safer. Devon ran his head over the top of his head. He'd cut his locs off, finally shedding the last vestiges of his prison stay. What would Keisha would think of it?

He jumped out of the car and headed to her front door. Devon looked around, noticing there wasn't much happening in the area. No one hanging out or walking along the neat streets. Keisha answered the door as soon as he knocked.

She was stunning.

He released a breath at the same time his wolf slammed against his defenses. The black dress she wore was fitted to her curves, with spaghetti straps holding the whole thing up. The top cupped her breasts and basically offered them to him. She wasn't exactly what some would call voluptuous, but on her tall figure, the curves she had made her thick in all the right places.

Devon's hands shook as he held up the roses he'd bought for her. Her painted red lips parted as a beautiful smile covered her face. She turned and waved him into her apartment. Her hair was slicked back from her face and falling down her back in waves. The length of it swayed along with her hips, and his eyes tracked every movement as he followed her into the nice-sized kitchen.

"These are beautiful, Devon, thank you," she said as she set the crystal vase they came in onto the counter.

"They don't compare to you," he said, his eyes skimming her body.

She chuckled. "Well, thank you. You look amazing."

He looked down at his fit. He'd also worn all black, from the dress pants and shirt that was open at the collar to the suit jacket he wore on top. He'd gone to the mall right after his meeting with Declan to make sure he could match his mate's fly.

Her fingers danced over his head. "You cut your hair." Her voice had a breathless quality that told him she liked it. She cupped his cheek. "I don't want to gas up your head, but you look fine as hell."

He laughed and rubbed his cheek against hers.

"Let's go. I'm excited to see where you're taking me," she told him, stepping back.

He smiled and preceded her out the door, turning around as she was locking up. "I don't like you on the bottom floor. I can't believe Silas allowed it."

"He's my boss, not my damn daddy," she said, rolling her eyes.

He stepped closer to her and gripped her chin gently, leaning down until barely a breath separated their lips. "Always rolling your eyes at me. I feel like you be dismissing me a lil bit."

"Noted," she said softly.

He couldn't resist a small kiss, pulling back before he could get carried away. He helped her into the Charger, closing the door after her. They made the drive to the restaurant in silence, and Devon found himself a little nervous. Would she like what he'd done for her? He pulled up to the restaurant he'd reserved, handing his keys off to the valet. He helped Keisha out of the car, and she looked at him in excitement.

"I've been wanting to come here for a while," she said, clapping softly.

They walked in, and the maître d' greeted them. Keisha gasped as she looked around.

The place was empty. She spun in a circle, her sharp gaze going back to him. She was every bit her father's daughter. He could see the questions in her eyes and knew that only the presence of the maître d' was keeping her from asking them.

She held her silence as they were seated at their table and even as a waitress came up with the wine he'd already ordered. He nodded at the woman to pour for them both.

The moment they were alone, Keisha quirked an eyebrow. "How exactly are you affording this?"

He chuckled. "I'm only gonna answer because you're my mate. Declan is gifted. He turned all the money I made from my prior profession into money that will take care of you and our kids."

She choked on the wine as she was taking a sip. "Kids, huh?"

"Ain't no use in me beating around the bush with you, shawty."

She looked away, unable to keep eye contact with his intense stare. "I don't know that I'm ready to change what I have going on to mate."

"I ain't ask you to change yet, mamas."

She narrowed her eyes and turned back to him.

He laughed. "Don't look at me like that. You finna start projecting all them corny ass dudes you dated before onto me and I ain't having it. I'm a grown ass man, my baby."

She gave him a look of disbelief, and he just chuckled. Wasn't nothing he could do but show her that he was serious, and he had plans to do just that, starting with their date tonight.

10...

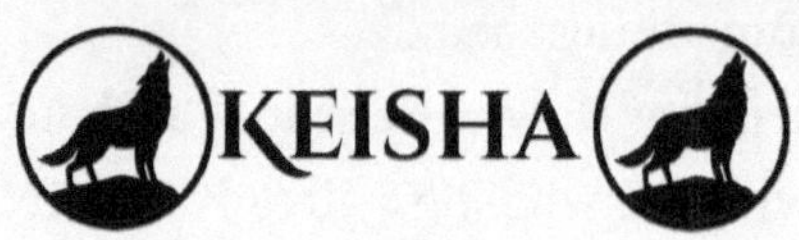

Keisha swirled wine around in her glass and studied Devon. He looked like he meant the words that he'd given her. But experience had taught her that anyone could say anything. She would wait to see what his actions said.

"What are you going to do now that you're out of prison?" She asked the question that was on the top of her head.

"I was just talking to my brother about that. I'm exploring my options." He shrugged.

Keisha hummed because that could mean anything. She debated asking her next question because she didn't know how she would react if he lied to her.

"I heard you were involved in a drive-by yesterday." She waited with bated breath on his answer.

He sighed. "As you can see, I'm whole and unharmed."

She sucked her teeth because that was not what she wanted to hear. "Do you plan to be in those types of situations now that you're out of prison?"

"I'm not on that, love."

She could read the sincerity in his eyes, so she nodded. "You know I work with Silas Knight?" He nodded. "Well, I don't want to speak out of turn, but I overheard them talking about your brother." She looked around and leaned closer. "He wants the tri-council seat for the wolves."

He waited her out, and she searched his face to see how he was reacting to what she told him.

"Ask your question, baby girl. I ain't hiding shit from you."

She sighed and sat back, lifting her glass for another sip. "If it's true, then you're likely to be his choice for his second."

He nodded and waved for her to continue her train of thought.

"Have you considered what it would be like in the Motsi?" She'd seen firsthand how the shifters in that society acted, and while there were a few people she knew that were down to earth, the others were petty and snobby. Not her type of crowd.

"Gotta be better than the streets," he said with a shrug.

"At least they're honest in the streets," she murmured.

He laughed again. "Key, what you want me to do, ma? You don't want me slinging, and you don't want me in the Motsi."

She sighed. "You can't do like me and get a regular, boring job?"

"Now who's trying to change who?"

She gasped, properly chastised. "I'm sorry."

"Nothing to apologize for. From that, I'm getting that you want security. There's nothing wrong with that."

She took a shaky breath. "I just…"

"Growing up as Leland's daughter couldn't have been easy," he said softly.

She shook her head. "I didn't want for anything, daddy made sure of it, but that uncertainty… It's burned into my soul," she admitted, and he grabbed her hand, pulling it to his lips.

"Tomorrow ain't promised, but I can promise that you and our jits will always be taken care of."

She growled and took her hand back. "I don't want money. I can make my own money. I want my mate at my side."

He nodded. "That's fair," he said, grimacing.

"It's why I left the old neighborhood. I'm not trying to be in a relationship where at any moment, the police could come knocking at my door about my mate."

"No one can guarantee you that, Key," he said, exasperated.

She knew that logically, but emotionally, it was hard to reconcile it. He looked off for a moment before turning to her.

"I took a vocational course for air conditioning maintenance and some electronics courses while I was locked up."

She gave him wide eyes. "Really? Did you like it?" She got comfortable in her chair, happy to talk about something else. It was a tacit agreement to agree to disagree, and she would take it for now.

"I did, surprisingly. My brother built me a workshop with the new house, so I've been in there messing around."

"Doing what?" she asked.

He laughed. "Believe it or not, I've been tinkering with some remote-control race cars. I'm going to eventually work on other shit, but for right now, I'm just having fun."

She smiled, liking this side of him. He looked relaxed, almost boyish as he explained to her how fast he was making the cars. Dinner passed with light conversation, for which she was happy. She hadn't wanted to ruin their date, but she needed him to understand where she was coming from.

After dinner, she clapped in giddy happiness as they pulled up to the theater. She gave him wide eyes as she saw what was playing. He chuckled at her expression.

"You said fancy, my love. Have you ever been to an opera?" he asked.

She shook her head. She'd never made the time for it, though she'd been to two ballets. The dates that had taken her had managed to ruin the experience both times by complaining. Her problem before had been that she wanted fancy things, but she wanted them from men who were rough around the edges. She hoped Devon wouldn't be the same.

She held up her hand for Devon to help her out of the car as he came around to her side.

"I got the best seats, according to the internet, which I would've thought were in the front but are not. I got us center seats."

The heels she wore put them almost at even height. She leaned over and kissed his cheek. "I'm so excited."

"Let's go then, mamas."

Almost three hours later, they were back outside at the valet counter. Devon accepted his coat back from Keisha as they waited for the valet to bring his car around. It had been cold inside the theater.

"It was beautiful," she told him softly. "This whole night was." She wrapped her arms around his waist. "Thank you for not complaining during the show."

She knew he'd asked her not to compare him to her other dates, but he didn't know how much it meant to her how great he was.

He lifted her chin and kissed her softly. "It was dope. Dude was obsessed with shawty. I should take it as a cautionary tale."

She laughed. "A word."

He helped her into his car and drove her home. Parking in front of her unit, he turned to her.

"Would you like to come in?" She held her breath.

The stare he gave her was intense. His eyes flashed a moment before he nodded. Keisha's small smile bloomed into a larger one, taking over her whole face. Her cheeks ached. She didn't want to come off thirsty, but…it had been a while for her.

Devon opened her door for her, holding out his hand. Accepting it, she guided them inside her apartment. Kicking off her shoes at the door, she rolled her shoulders, shaking off some of her nervousness.

"Would you like something to drink?"

Devon kept his body still, afraid to move for fear he would attack his mate. He wanted gentle for their first time, but the molten need firing his bloodstream probably wouldn't allow for it. He'd spent the last two years of his bid celibate, despite the opportunities that had been thrown at him. The last time he'd had sex was with a nurse in the prison clinic, and the ensuing mess had almost fucked up his freedom. He'd kept his dick to himself after that, counting down the days until he left.

He pushed his wolf down, begging patience from it. He knew Keisha wasn't ready to mate, so the knotting the animal craved wouldn't happen tonight. But he would use this time to savor her, and Devon was looking forward to it. Still...

Waves of dominance pushed through his body, his power flaring out of his control as he watched her. She turned around to see why he hadn't answered her question. Her soft gasp sent chills through his body.

"Is that a yes or no?" she asked quietly.

The sway of her hips as she walked slowly to him hypnotized him. The power of her animal reached him before she did, the she-wolf prodding at his aura. If he had any doubts about their mating before, it was gone now. The very fact that their animals were both invested, their power blending and flowing in and out of them as Keisha stepped closer... He almost felt like if he closed his eyes, he would be able to see their power dancing together. She didn't stop until the tips of her breasts pressed into his chest. His body shuddered, hard. Unvarnished and urgent desire slammed into him.

Words were lost to him. What could he say to a goddess anyway? Nothing would come close to describing the lust making him tremble. He grabbed the back of her neck, lowering his head slowly.

"Kiss me, love." He meant for it to be a request, but the soft growl was filled with dominance.

The sound around him dimmed as he awaited her response. The only thing he could hear was the drumming of his pulse in his ears. He'd never wanted a kiss more in his life. Finally, after an interminable wait, Keisha went up on her toes and sealed their mouths together. Her lips parted on a satisfied sigh and Devon took advantage, swiping his tongue inside.

She sucked on his tongue, hungrily kissing him. He didn't push for more, instead delighting in the pleasure of his mate. Her body softened the longer they kissed, her muscles relaxing beneath his hands. Devon pulled back to breathe, cupping her chin. He held her there until her lids finally lifted. The smoldering lust in her gaze had his thumb trembling as he traced her bottom lip.

"I want to be gentle, sweetheart, but it's been so long, and my wolf will be greedy with you." He grimaced as the animal swiped at his body in renewed impatience.

Her hands cupped his cheeks, her claws growing against his skin. "I didn't ask for gentle," she said softly. "We're not ready for your bite, but she doesn't want easy either."

A hungry growl rattled his chest. "Be sure," he demanded.

Keisha went up on her toes and butted her forehead against his. "*You* be sure."

It was a challenge to his wolf and the animal answered immediately, slamming against Devon's shields. His next kiss had none of the gentleness of before. It was greedy and aggressive, their tongues clashing, little nips and bites drawing blood. Keisha moaned into his mouth. Taking it as assent, he lifted her legs, wrapping them around his waist. He didn't let up his kiss as he followed her scent to her bedroom.

Spinning their bodies, Devon sat on the edge of her bed. He slapped her ass and leaned back.

"Clothes off, love." His gruff order spurred her from his lap. "Slow," was his next demand.

He licked his lips and watched, knowing he was pushing it. His animal was already on edge and watching her reveal her curves was a torturous tease. He shed his shirt but left his pants on and open. He gripped his dick as his mate turned her back to him before sliding her dress down her body.

Good God.

Her impish smile as she turned to face him had his dick leaking. Keisha's gaze strayed down to his erection, her tongue darting out to swipe at her lips. He wanted her mouth on him in the worst way, but that would have to wait. He needed inside her. He stood and shed his pants, pulling her into his arms. He turned them again, pushing her back onto the bed. He had every intention of diving inside his mate, but then she opened her legs and his mouth started watering for the taste of her.

He dragged her ass to the edge of the bed and went to his knees. Keisha whimpered as he licked across the folds of her sex. Devon devoured her, wallowing in her taste. His wolf prodded him, demanding he take even more. She screamed, her pussy clenching around his fingers as she came, and still, he kept going, ravenous for her. Another orgasm rocked her and still, he ate at her.

"Dev," she begged hoarsely.

He lifted from his new favorite treat, kissing his way up her legs.

"I already know I'm gonna be addicted to this shit," he murmured before kissing her.

Devon fit her legs into the crooks of his elbows, opening her wide for his pleasure. Her breath hitched as he slid his dick across her folds.

"Ready, love?" He couldn't help the strain in his voice.

He was on the precipice of what he knew would be the greatest pussy of his life, and it was taking everything in him to keep from slamming forward. Keisha nodded, lifting her hips in invitation. The wanton smile she gave him sent a hard shudder through his body. This was a woman who knew the power she would hold over him. She would be hell, and he would dive headfirst into the fires just to have her.

She reached her hand down and guided him to her opening, her greedy pussy sucking him in. Even with her pulling him in, her walls clenched around him, pushing against his invasion. He pulled back, making his strokes shallow.

"Let me in, mamas," he cajoled.

She nodded, her mouth dropping open as he finally pushed all the way in. He hissed as the pleasure shook him. The first full push was the only gentle stroke he could manage. His next one was harder and deeper as he lost himself in the rhythm of their bodies. Devon lifted her hips from the bed, gripping her tightly. It was a different angle, and the moan Keisha released told him he was hitting the exact spot he wanted to hit. She chanted his name as he stroked into her. The way her body squeezed down on him, Devon was a goner.

Sweat coated their bodies and time ceased to mean anything as he drove his mate up and then over the precipice. He cursed in relief, ready to follow her. His toes curled and his body stiffened as he came. His wolf howled as his power covered her. He held her hips tight against him as he released everything that had been building up inside of him.

It was a full minute before he could stop his body from trembling. He settled her gently, laying on her for a moment while he caught his breath. He hoped she had no plans for tomorrow because there was no way he was done with her tonight.

11...

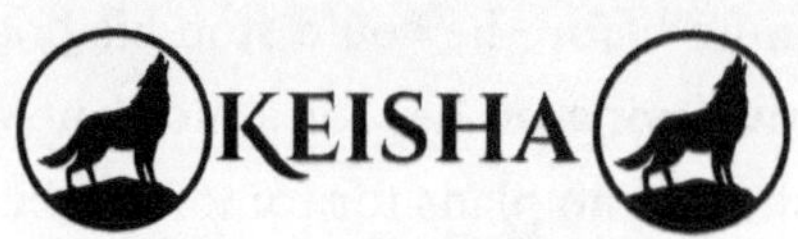

Even a week after her first date with Devon, Keisha was still on a high. The date had gone great and the two of them talked more than once a day. Devon was giving a full court press and she liked it. Right now, she was sitting at her mother's kitchen table eating breakfast, debating whether or not to tell her. The two of them talked about damn near everything. Ever since her father had died, she and Patrice had grown tighter.

She looked out into the backyard where the new gazebo caught her attention. Silas had come through, and she would remind herself to thank him. She'd completely forgotten about it since dealing with Devon. Losing details like that was so unlike her.

"The gazebo really looks nice. Mr. Knight said he would send someone over. How much did they end up charging you?"

Her mother smiled. "I didn't pay anything."

Keisha whipped her head toward Patrice. "What?"

"My son-in-law arranged everything. He wouldn't let me lift a finger."

"Son-in-law?" she snapped. "Devon been over here? When?"

She was honestly shocked. It wasn't like she needed to introduce the two of them. Devon had worked for her father for years, so Patrice knew him well. But, like…well enough for him to just come over? Plus, it was very presumptuous of him to…

Keisha paused and shook her head, releasing the breath she was holding. Getting worked up over nothing was silly. She was supposed to be giving him a chance, and getting offended at everything was not the way to do that.

Patrice was studying her. "I envy you that trick."

Keisha blinked. "What?"

"The way you work through problems on the spot. I can almost see the thoughts going around in your mind as you piece through them. I wish I could do that."

"There's no problem. You just caught me off guard."

"Hmm," was all her mother said.

"He told you I was his mate?"

"Outright claimed you," Patrice told her.

Keisha tried to hide her smile.

"Are you happy?"

"Mmhmm. Apprehensive also," Keisha admitted.

Her mother nodded. "That's fair. He told me he was getting out of the game completely. That's a good sign to me."

He'd told her the same, but a part of her was still worried. Her father had made the same promises to her mother, but by the time he'd gotten out, he was killed a year later. Leaving never promised safety.

"Did you believe him?" She held her breath because she trusted her mother's opinion.

"He seemed serious. The plans his brother has will keep him busy, but no safer, probably." Patrice sighed.

Keisha's heart knocked against her chest. Her mother was right, and she felt a little validated because she knew it was dangerous. Devon didn't seem to understand that. Her phone rang and she bit her lip. Speak of the devil. She picked it up.

"Hey, mamas. What are you doing?"

"Having breakfast with mama, then I'm taking her to the grocery store," she answered.

"I want to spend time with you."

He was so upfront, she couldn't control the smile that tilted her lips. "I can call you afterward."

"You at your mom's?"

"Yep."

"Okay, bet. Don't leave without me," he said firmly.

"Devon, you don't have to—" The line went dead, and her mother smirked at her incredulous expression.

"Wolves," Patrice said on a chuckle.

Keisha sucked her teeth. "He will be sorely disappointed if he thinks he finna come in my life and take over."

Patrice scoffed. "Don't let your stubbornness make your mating more difficult than it needs to be."

"I'm too grown to change," Keisha muttered.

"He's a good man, KeKe." Patrice chastised. "Even when he was locked up, he looked out for us."

"What?" Surprise had her sitting back in her seat.

"I wouldn't take his money, but it didn't stop him from making sure we were safe. And he got you an interview with Silas Knight. He good in my book, always."

"What?!" Her voice went up a couple octaves.

"I told him you wanted to come home and needed a job for that to happen. He called me within hours, having fixed it."

Keisha sat stunned. She remembered thinking how fast everything had happened, from the time she'd called her mother to the time she had the interview and then the job. She didn't know how to feel about what her mother was telling her. Once upon a time, Patrice hadn't wanted anything to do with her father's business nor the people he associated with. When had she made an exception for Devon? Had it been after she told Patrice that she suspected he was her mate?

"Devon's calls to check on us allowed me to get to know him more," Patrice explained.

"He called you from prison?"

Patrice nodded. "Let me go get dressed so I can be ready when he gets here. Clean the kitchen," she ordered, leaving Keisha sitting alone.

As she cleaned their breakfast dishes and wiped down the counters, her mother's words were chasing themselves around in her mind. What else had Devon done that she hadn't known about? Had he already known they were mates? The doorbell rang as she was finishing up. She rushed to the front, snatching the door open.

"Did you get me my job?"

Devon grabbed her waist and guided her inside, nuzzling against her neck. "Good morning, love."

He kissed her softly right under her ear, and she shuddered as her body flushed with heat. Keisha sighed as he pecked her lips with little kisses until her mouth opened for him. He delved his tongue inside and pulled her into his frame. It was like a switch flipped as her whole body relaxed into his. He pulled back and gave her a smug smile.

"Good morning," she managed to whisper, her eyes fluttering.

"To answer your question, I called Silas when I found out you were looking for a job. But he wouldn't have hired you if you didn't show up and show out at the interview."

That made her feel better. She kissed the hollow of his neck where she could reach, licking against his skin. He smelled amazing, and now that she wasn't fake mad at him, she could think of better things to do with their time.

"Where's ma?" he asked, cupping her ass.

She rolled her eyes and stepped back. "Oh, it's *ma*, now?"

He chuckled. "You the only one playing around, my baby. Me and mama are of one accord."

"Hey, baby!" Patrice called as she came down the hall.

Devon mushed her forehead to move her out of the way and went to hug her mama. She sucked her teeth at them both because they were doing the most.

"Have you eaten anything today, Devon?" Patrice asked.

"God almighty," Keisha muttered. "Mama, come on before these stores get packed."

"I'm good, ma. I'm here to drive my two beautiful women around today," he told her.

"I was going to drive," Keisha interjected.

Both of them ignored her. Patrice grabbed her purse and linked her arm with Devon's, walking past Keisha. She could only sigh as she locked her mother's door.

Devon eased Patrice into the front seat of his Range Rover, and Keisha knew she was in for a long day. He held the back door for her, the amused smirk on his face telling her everything she needed to know. She barely kept from rolling her eyes.

"What's the matter, my baby?"

She did roll her eyes this time. "I can already tell y'all both finna get on my nerves."

Devon gripped her chin and nipped her bottom lip. "There you go, rolling your eyes."

Keisha sighed. "You not 'bout to run me, Devon."

"Oh, yeah?" The smile he gave her had her squirming in his back seat. "Buckle up, love," he ordered, waiting until she did before he closed the door.

As much as she wanted to resist Devon, he had a way about him that was giving her wolf everything she needed. That damned animal wanted someone who could take control of them, and Keisha had to admit she liked it too.

12

Devon hummed along to the R&B coming out of his speakers. He'd had a good day with his mate and her mother. He and Ms. Patrice chatted the entire time, Keisha only interjecting when she felt like they were taking too long. It had been comforting to do something that felt normal, from sneaking kisses with his mate in between aisles to Ms. Patrice's attempts to mother him. She asked him questions about his childhood and what his current likes were foodwise.

The whole day left him feeling warm and welcomed. It was close to nine in the evening as he pulled out of Ms. Patrice's neighborhood, full from the dinner she'd made them. He had a couple of moves to make, or he would've talked his mate into coming with him. Speaking of which, he pulled up Tangie's number. She answered quickly.

"You heading here?"

"Yep. Be there in like ten. We need to talk."

She hummed. "See you soon, then."

His day with Keisha and her mother was reinforcing his need to see Tangie. The more he thought about the years he'd missed with his mate, his desire to find out if it truly was a setup rose. He understood the shit he'd been doing was illegal, but he was never sloppy with it. And for the most part, humans didn't give a fuck what shifters did, so what had set them onto his trail? Add to that Leland dying within months, and it was all looking funny in the light.

He pulled into Tangie's driveway and her garage door lifted. He drove inside, glad that their meeting would be private. It reminded him that he needed to introduce Keisha to Tangie. He didn't want any misunderstandings when it came to his mate.

He got out, smiling when he saw his friend waiting for him at her kitchen door. His smile dimmed when he saw what she was wearing. The white tank top was small, the shorts even more so. A part of him wondered if it was because she was comfortable with him, but there was a little warning in the back of his head that told him to tread carefully.

"My neighbors too damn nosy," she told him as he walked up.

He kissed her forehead. "Discreet is always better."

She nodded and led him inside. He kept his eyes on his surroundings and not the way her curvy figure filled the barely-there shorts as he followed her into her living room. Her place was neat, even though he could see the touches of her son all over the house. Dinosaur toys littered the floor. He smiled as he sat down on the sofa, grabbing a stuffed animal.

"Where's T-Rex?" he asked, using her nickname for her dinosaur-obsessed son.

She smiled softly. "With my grandmother. She likes to take him overnight when there's no school."

"Talk to me, Tang," Devon ordered, changing the subject now that he knew they wouldn't be interrupted.

"What do you want to know?" She sat next to him and turned her body his way.

"Tell me about the male you were dating at the time. Is he Theo's father?"

Her eyes widened and guilt filled them before she turned her head. Devon's mind drifted back to that night. They were both in Tangie's boyfriend's car when they were pulled over by the police. There was a bag of drugs in the trunk. Tangie swore up and down she hadn't known the drugs were there.

"Why are you bringing it up now?" There was curiosity in her tone.

"I think it was all a setup." He studied her face. "The jail time, Leland's death. All of it."

She frowned. "No one knew you would be in the car with me. How could that part be a setup?"

His eyes narrowed because it wasn't quite a denial. "Could your ex be involved?"

She looked uncomfortable.

"I'm not blaming you, Tangie. It seems like the shit was bigger than the both of us. Who were you messing with?"

"Marcus Cartwright."

"The fuck?" Devon leaned back against the sofa cushions. "Arthur's son? What was he doing in our neck of the woods?" He went through his memories, trying to remember if he'd ever seen the wolf in this part of town.

Arthur Cartwright was a member of the tri-council before Cyrus Booth. Cyrus had killed him when he took over the seat. According to the old heads in the neighborhood, it had been brutal. It wasn't something he'd paid attention to because it hadn't meant shit to him.

"Where would he have gotten access to the amount of work that was in that bag? The math ain't mathing on that, Tang." Devon shook his head.

He'd been booked for intent to distribute along with possession, which meant that there were a lot of drugs. Most of that night was hazy to him due to how much he'd drank, but the charges they'd read at his arraignment… He'd been shocked, to say the least.

She sighed. "I know. Marcus wasn't…that's not the type of person he was. Maybe we weren't the target. Maybe he was."

Devon pinched the bridge of his nose. He had to concede that to her because Tangie was driving her boyfriend's car that night, so, like she'd said, there was no way anyone could've known Devon would be in that car with her beforehand.

He thought back to that night. The only reason he'd been riding with Tangie was because he'd gotten drunk at a party and Delilah, his girlfriend at the time, had left him, mad at some bullshit, per usual. He didn't remember much from that night, just waking up hung over in a jail cell. When they told him what he'd admitted to, he stood on it because the alternative was a pregnant Tangie going to prison. He couldn't allow a child to grow up the way he and his brother had. He shook his head.

"Maybe Councilman Booth wanted to get rid of the Cartwright line altogether," she posited. "Marcus told me that his father used to work with Leland when he was councilman. I don't know, Dev." She shook her head and shrugged. "When they killed Marcus, I...I wasn't in the headspace to deal with any of this. But now that you're home and safe, I can help you put the pieces together."

"Could be dangerous, Tang. I don't know if I want you involved."

She scoffed. "I'm grown, Dev. A whole ass mother."

"Exactly my point."

"You can't stop me." She lifted her chin and stared him down.

Devon sighed and lifted his hands. "It's all good, Tang. I'm just trying to make sure none of this shit comes back to bite my brother in the ass."

"I understand that." She scooted closer to him until their legs touched.

He looked down, his wolf aggravated at her nearness. To keep from saying something rude, he changed the subject. "So, when am I going to meet Theo formally?"

"Soon. Theo will be happy to meet the person feeding his toy addiction in person." She laughed and rubbed her hand down his arm. "Now, what have you been doing now that you're out? Picking up with old relationships?"

He frowned. "What you mean?"

She smiled and tucked her straight hair behind her ear. "You know what I mean. Ten years in prison, Devon. I know you ready to take the edge off. Who's the lucky woman?"

"I met my mate," he told her, standing to put distance between them.

Tangie stood after him, a frown on her face. She inhaled deeply. "A mate? When? You've barely been out and your scent hasn't changed since I last saw you."

"I met her the night I got out." He smiled. "You remember Keisha Calhoun?"

"Wow, that's…" She tugged down on the bottom of her tank top. "Leland's daughter. Ms. Patrice won't allow that." She chuckled dryly.

"I spent the day with them both. It'll all work out the way it's supposed to." The silence that descended was thick with an unnamed tension.

"I thought…" She sighed. "Did you even interact with her before you went to jail? Did she hold you down while you were inside the way I did?"

Devon frowned. "What are you talking about? We both know you did that out of guilt," he reminded her.

Tangie flinched. "That's not completely true. I just… I thought we were building something."

Devon studied his friend in confusion. Where had any of this come from? He'd made her no promises while inside. Hell, their conversations were strictly about her son and his daily life. Had he given her any indication that he would be with her when he was released?

Instead of standing around and figuring it out, Devon headed toward the kitchen door. "You should leave that other matter to me, Tangie. I don't want you involved."

"Wait, you don't have to go." She rushed after him. "We can chill. I'm not going to disrespect your new mating."

"Nah, I need to get home. Call me when you're ready for me to meet Theo," he told her.

"I will."

He quickly escaped the awkwardness, his wolf irritated by the fact that another woman had tried to move into his mate's space. The drive back to his house was made with the music low as he went through everything they'd talked about. Could the setup be that extensive? He didn't think something like that could go on under his nose and he not hear about it.

His eyes narrowed on his rearview mirror as he turned onto the interstate. There was a car following him. Instead of going home, he sped and slipped into the right lane, then off the next exit. The car recklessly did the same, confirming his suspicion.

He knew the West side like the back of his hand, so he zipped through the city streets with them on his ass. Reaching into his middle console, Devon pulled out his 9mm, sliding it into his lap as the light in front of him turned red. The dark car made a move to come up on the side of him, but a minivan cut them off and pulled up next to Devon. He glanced at the family in the car and cursed. If the car behind him decided to get active, he didn't want the family next to him to get caught in the crossfire.

Fuck it.

He ran the red light, chuckling at the cacophony of horns from angry motorists. The car didn't follow, so he quickly found the nearest interstate entrance and got back on, speeding away. He took the long way to his house and breathed a sigh of relief as he pulled the truck into his garage. Sitting in the dark, he debated his next move. Had they followed him from Tangie's house, or had they been tailing him since he'd been with his mate?

He shook his head because he would've noticed if someone had been following him around with Keisha in the car. His wolf was hyper-vigilant when she was with him. That meant they'd followed him from Tangie's. He would need to holla at Julian. Some shit was going on.

13...

Once or twice a month, Keisha made time to spend with her cousins on her mother's side. The panthers were a tight-knit bunch, and her cousins always openly embraced her. Despite her boss's claim that she didn't take any time off, Keisha made time for her cousins, always. To that end, she'd picked up Lucky at her house on the South side, and they were headed to this popping brunch spot that straddled the two territories.

"I'm glad you driving because after the week I've had, these bottomless mimosas about to hit." Lucky pulled down the visor and added more lip gloss to her full, painted red lips. Her hair was down her back in two fishtail braids. The sundress her cousin wore dipped low in the front.

"I hope you got them thangs tied down because two drinks in and they gon' pop out that dress," Keisha joked.

Lucky snickered. "Don't do me."

She opened her mouth to tease her again when her phone rang. She smiled seeing Devon's name across the dash. Despite the hard time she'd given him and her mother, she'd had a great time yesterday. She mostly dreaded grocery shopping on the weekends, but he'd made it fun.

"Hey, Devon," she greeted.

"What you up to today?" The way his voice filled the car sent a shiver through her.

"Hanging out with my cousin Lucky."

He grunted. "All day?"

"Maybe," she hedged, and he chuckled. She wanted to see him, but lord knows that man didn't need his ego stroked. "We're doing brunch and then hitting up the mall. I have to buy a dress for a work event."

"Damn, and you ain't invite me?"

She smiled. "You want to go to a boring fundraiser with me?" She fought to keep the surprise from her voice.

Devon growled. "I feel like you trying to say something, Key."

She laughed. "I'm not. I just didn't figure you'd want to go to something like that."

"I'm on what you on, mamas. Didn't I take your ass to an opera?"

She couldn't help the smile that spread across her face. "You right, that's my bad."

"Pull up on me," he ordered.

She checked the time and rolled her eyes. "Where are you? I gotta get to brunch for our reservation."

"I'll send you my location. It won't take but a minute, love." He hung up, and she sucked her teeth.

"He act like his word is law," she muttered.

Lucky laughed. "Shit, he said he on what you on." She raised her hands to the roof. "Lord, I see what you've done for others..."

Keisha cracked up. "You doing too much."

"From what Auntie told me, you better quit playing," her cousin said.

Keisha got a ding with the address and let out a sigh of relief. He wasn't too far from where she needed to be, so she could swing it. That was the only reason she was following his orders.

Right.

That's what she told herself.

Pulling up to the older neighborhood, she looked around. It wasn't quite across the tracks, but it was close enough for her to be worried about what he was doing here. He told her and her mother that he was leaving the streets behind, so she didn't understand why he was hanging out in these parts. She saw his car parked along the curb in front of a house and pulled in behind it. Her breath caught as she finally spotted him.

Devon came down off the porch, his swagger sending her pulse racing. She swallowed hard when he made his way to her.

"Girl, he walk like he toting—"

"Alright now," Keisha cut her cousin off.

"Shit, just saying."

As he came over to the driver's side, Keisha lowered the window. He leaned down and spoke. "Nice to meet you, Lucky."

"Same to you, cousin-in-law," Lucky simpered.

Devon smirked, exposing the gold slugs on his bottom teeth. *Lord have mercy.* She squirmed in her seat.

"Out the car, Key."

She wished she could say it aggravated her, but her clit jumped at his command and disobeying him never crossed her mind. He stepped back and she opened the door, sighing in pleasure as he pulled her into his arms.

"I missed you," he murmured against her lips, kissing her.

"You just saw me yesterday. But you could've asked nicely and I would've come to see you after I was done."

"Oh, I have to ask nicely?" He chuckled against her neck.

"You should try it sometime," she teased.

Devon smiled and nipped her lip. He grabbed her ass and brought her closer. She tried to look around, to see who he was hanging out with, but he moved his head to block her line of sight. She was worried about him falling into old habits.

"What you doing out here?"

He gripped her chin. "You worried about the wrong thing." He kissed her deeply and it clouded her mind, making her forget her follow-up question.

He stepped back and spun her in a circle. "You look fly as hell, mamas."

Her cheeks heated. She wore a denim corset with a short floral swing skirt that swirled around her thighs as he twirled her. Her high heels clicked as she turned back to him. His hand traced her thighs and she shuddered. It reminded her of their date night. It was nearly a week later and she could still feel the remnants of his touch on her body.

Devon stepped back and pulled his wallet out, handing her a platinum card with the logo of an exclusive bank that serviced the town's richest residents. She frowned and glanced at it, her eyebrows pulling deeper when she noticed her name on it. She looked up at him in surprise.

"Devon..." she started.

"Would you rather I pull a knot out of my pocket every time you or mama need something?"

"It's not your responsibility to take care of us." Even as she said the words, butterflies fluttered in her stomach and her wolf moved through her body, her emotions rising.

He sucked his teeth. "Quit playing with me, shawty."

Lord, this man. The care he showed her would have her falling in love with him despite her every intention to take their relationship slow. She opened her mouth to argue, but he tilted her chin up and leaned in.

"You finna argue with me and I ain't having it. Now, go on and get out the street." He kissed her lightly.

"Thank you," she whispered.

"I already told you what it is with me, Key. You gotta let loose some of that control."

She nodded, not agreeing or disagreeing. He chuckled and shook his head, kissing her again.

"Come see me when you're done." His soft order pleased her wolf, and Keisha's chin notched higher on instinct in submission.

The cocky smile exposed his golds, and Keisha sighed with the realization that she just might be a bird. Here she was telling this man to get out the streets and get a regular ass job, but everything about him from his rough swagger to the Cuban links lying against his black t-shirt turned her on. His nostrils flared as he inhaled deeply.

"Alright, mamas," he muttered, caging her throat with his rough hands. "Behave, or you gon' be missing brunch with your girls."

Keisha nodded again, on mute and seriously considering abandoning her cousins. He turned her around, his hand still around her neck. The steel of his erection pressed against her ass, and it took everything in her to keep upright on her shaky legs. He was bossy and domineering and damn if it didn't push every one of her buttons. Devon kissed her softly below her ear.

"Have fun, and be safe," he whispered.

She was in a daze as he helped her into her front seat, closing the door on her. He tapped the car and stepped back. Her hands shook as she buckled her seat belt.

Lucky fanned her face. "Bitch."

Keisha sighed as she pulled off. "I know, chile. That man fine as fuck, and so much trouble."

Her cousin snickered. "That's why auntie told you not to come up off that man."

She sucked her teeth and rolled her eyes. "Your auntie get on my nerves. She 'bout to spoil that man before I even get a chance."

Three hours after she left her mate, Keisha was still thinking about him. Which was probably his intention. She was supposed to go to the mall after this, but thoughts of pulling up on Devon consumed her. She had plenty of time to look for a dress for the fundraiser and she was pretty sure Lucky would understand. They'd had a blast at brunch, but hanging with her cousins was always fun.

By the time Lucky had finished embellishing as she told them about Devon, her cousins were deep into their pitcher of mimosas. Between the congratulations and the teasing, Keisha could only laugh. It had been a good afternoon.

She nibbled her bottom lip as she considered whether or not she'd call Devon while she waited for the valet to bring her car around. The hair on the back of her neck rose and her wolf rattled her chest in warning. Pulling her clutch close, Keisha looked around the crowded valet station. Her cousins were loud behind her, but she tuned them out to find out what was making her wolf uncomfortable.

She finally met a pair of glaring dark eyes. The dark-skinned beauty was stacked, her yellow bodycon dress emphasizing every curve. She sighed as the woman took Keisha's gaze for her signal to approach. All twenty-two inches of her hair swayed as she drew closer to Keisha, the wolf underneath the woman's skin making its presence known.

Keisha already knew what the bitch wanted and she'd warned Devon that she wasn't going to be putting up with people approaching her about him. The valet handed her her keys, but Keisha waited until the she-wolf reached her. She wasn't running from no bitch.

The woman sneered as she got closer. "He'll be running back to me when he tires of you, mate or not."

"You must be Delilah," Keisha said.

The woman preened as though Keisha knowing who she was proved something. "You think Devon will be faithful to you, but wolves only mate for one thing, and as soon as you pop out a kid for him, he'll be back. Ask your mother how it goes."

Keisha could've handled it better, she could admit that in hindsight, but perhaps it was the mention of her mama that set her off. She didn't know, but she did know she had no control over her hand as it snaked out and slapped the shit out of the woman.

"Let that be the last time you approach me about my mate. Tell all them other bitches too." Keisha kept her voice calm despite the anger roiling within her.

The she-wolf started to lunge, but Keisha grabbed Delilah around the throat, squeezing, just barely keeping her wolf from dropping its claws.

"And keep my mama's name out yo' mouth." She shoved her back, and Delilah tripped over her high heels and hit the ground.

Ignoring her cackling cousins, Keisha strutted around to the driver's side of her car, putting an extra sway to her hips as she got in. If she thought the teasing about her mating was bad before… The group chat was finna be relentless. Lucky snickered the moment they drove away.

"Don't even, Lucky," she grumbled.

"Didn't you give me the talk about fighting in the street before we left the house?"

Keisha laughed, shaking off her aggravation. "Because you don't know how to act."

"My cousin said, '*Tell them other bitches too.*'" Lucky cackled.

"I can't stand you."

Lucky whipped out her phone and Keisha made a grab for it.

"Don't be putting it in the group chat," she fussed.

"Too late." Lucky's shoulders were shaking with mirth. "Rocky dropped a video in there."

Keisha groaned because she knew Patrice was finna act up. Her phone rang and her eyes widened. Lord, that was fast. She relaxed when she realized it was Devon.

"Key," he said when she connected the call.

"Yes?"

"I said you could slap people up and down this city, but I didn't think you would take that seriously."

Her eyes narrowed. "That bitch called you?" She was about to get rude if he was taking calls from other women.

"I don't even know who you're talking about, ma. I don't deal with any other women."

"Then how you know what I'm doing?"

"I'm gon' always know what you doing," he volleyed back.

"You called to fuss at me for slapping one of your hoes?" Her wolf was riled at the thought.

"Key," he growled in warning, and her wolf sat forward, obedient and anxious. "I called to check on you."

"Oh."

Lucky snickered next to her.

"Yeah. Oh," he said and hung up.

Keisha sighed. God, now she had to apologize to him.

"You in *trouble*," Lucky sang.

"Shut up," she snapped, rolling her eyes as Lucky laughed again.

She was a nervous wreck by the time she parked at the Eastfield Luxury Plaza. Should she try and call Devon back and apologize or wait until later? She wasn't a person to let shit linger, but he was a hard man to figure out. If it was any of the other relationships she'd had before, she wouldn't care, but Patrice's words came back to her. She didn't want to make her mating harder than it had to be.

Lucky elbowed her in the side as they approached the entrance to the mall. Devon was standing there, legs apart, arms crossed over his chest, his dark eyes laser-focused on her. Keisha's heart thumped against her chest. How did he even know where to find her?

She couldn't read his expression, but people entering the mall parted around him as though they could sense the predator lurking inside. His energy was potent, so she could only imagine the power his wolf was giving off that had people avoiding being near him.

"Now that's a man," Lucky whispered as they approached him.

Her wolf swiped at her in displeasure and Keisha already knew what the animal wanted. "I'm sorry for the way I spoke to you," she said as soon as they got close enough.

He lifted her chin and inspected her face before nodding. "Ain't but one woman got a claim to me, so fighting other bitches 'bout me is dead, hear?"

She nodded quickly, her stomach clenching in lust.

Lucky cleared her throat, and the tension swimming around them lessened. "Devon, if you're here while we're shopping, that means the tab's on you."

His eyes never left Keisha's, and she shuddered as his tongue swiped across his bottom lip.

"You finna run my pockets, cousin?" he directed to Lucky.

"And is," Lucky declared, hooking her arm through his.

Devon dropped a soft kiss to Keisha's lips before turning away to focus on her cousin. He spun himself and Lucky around to face the mall. She released the breath she was holding, feeling deprived of his presence though he was still close. She ran a shaky hand over the top of her head and reset.

"I draw the line at carrying bags. You gotta lug around whatever you buy," he told Lucky.

"You must don't know what I do for a living," Lucky joked, dragging him through the door.

Keisha sucked her teeth at her cousin. "Girl, you ride around in a mail truck, you ain't lugging big packages," she teased.

Lucky stuck her tongue out at Keisha. "Your mate's a hater, Devon."

He laughed, and Keisha bid her heart to slow down. She was falling in love with this man. Why it took him putting his foot down for her to realize it, she didn't know — and should probably sit on someone's couch to talk about it. But God, he knew how to handle her, and that was a major turn-on.

14...

Keisha was impatient as she unlocked her front door. Devon was nibbling on her neck, his hands roaming her breasts as she finally got the damn thing opened. Pushing inside, she locked it behind them before dropping to her knees in front of him. His eyes lit with his wolf, his growl filling the air around them.

He dropped his pants with no prodding from her, and Keisha licked her lips in anticipation. She grabbed his erection, wasting no time sliding her mouth down his hardness. Devon grabbed her hair, bunching the loose curls in his hand and holding her in place. She breathed through her nose as he touched the back of her throat. His hum of pleasure spurred her on, and Keisha gripped him tighter as she bobbed up and down his dick.

"Just like that, my baby," Devon coached, his hips moving in time with her.

She cupped his balls gently, smiling when Devon growled lower. Before she could get too smug, he snatched her off his dick, swinging her until she was against the wall. The bite of his power rained over her, little stings that prodded her wolf to respond. Her claws dropped and her animal wallowed in the wave of dominance pulsing off of him. Keisha's body shuddered, the hair on the nape of her neck rustling in anticipation.

Devon didn't make her wait long, ripping her panties off and driving into her. She screamed as he pushed through her clenching inner muscles, her nails digging into his shoulders. His wolf responded, and he fucked into her with rough strokes that had her body in flames. She prided herself on her independence, but under the right set of circumstances, she would happily submit to this man.

She bit her lip, moaning as he slid across her g-spot. Her wolf was begging her to bite him, to mark his body so that anyone who saw him knew who he belonged to. Keisha had never imagined she would be so possessive. She tucked her head into his neck, winding her hips, grinding her clit against his crotch. She sucked his skin into her mouth, leaving a dark enough mark to satisfy her animal.

"Almost there," she panted, reaching for the orgasm contracting her stomach.

She scraped her teeth against his neck and Devon fucked her harder, long, desperate strokes that had her seeing stars. His fingers left marks on her thighs as he gripped her tighter. Every stroke stole a little more of her air until she was holding her breath.

He put his stamp on her, claiming her without exchanging a single bite. Keisha went up in flames, her climax tightening her body. His shout of pleasure as he followed her over the edge bounced off the walls of her foyer.

"Fuck, woman," he finally managed to say.

His chest moved against hers as they both battled for air.

"If that's your idea of punishment, you may have just created a monster," she said lazily.

Devon chuckled, kissing her softly. "Shit, if you plan on putting your pussy on me like that, you can slap whoever the fuck you want to."

She laughed and hugged him closer, kissing one of the marks on his neck.

"You marked my shit up?"

"And did." She was entirely unrepentant.

He stepped out of his pants and walked them into her room, setting her down in the bathroom. Keisha walked over to the shower and started it. When she turned around, Devon was watching her.

"What?"

"Tell me the source of your insecurity. I don't mind fucking you up against any wall, but I don't want you walking around unsure of us."

She felt his sincerity. Sighing, she stepped into the shower to stall. He came in behind her, pulling her back into his stomach.

"Talk to me, mamas. The only way this works is if we communicate," he murmured against her skin.

She turned in his arms and studied him. "Did you know dad cheated on mom?"

Devon frowned. "What? They were mates, right?"

She growled low in aggravation, Delilah's words coming back to her. "Not every wolf shifter is monogamous. A lot of them take other lovers from time to time. It seems my father was one of those wolves."

Devon grunted but said nothing.

"When he died..." She shook her head. "You don't even want to know how many showed up to his funeral."

He pulled her into his arms. "I'm sorry you both went through that."

She was happy that he didn't try and invalidate her feelings. She'd been rightfully pissed when those women approached her mother, but her aunts had chided her to stay in a child's place. The onus was on her mother to be the bigger person and not make a scene. Keisha would not be living her life that way.

"I refuse to be made a fool," she told him adamantly.

Devon cupped her cheek and looked her dead in the eye. "I would never disrespect you like that. I swear."

Her wolf believed him, the animal moving through her body. Time would tell if the woman could trust him.

"If marking me makes you feel better, then have at it," he told her, kissing her. "I know when I bite you, that shit gon' be seen from a mile away."

She laughed, her body relaxing. "Stay the night?"

"That was a given," he said arrogantly.

Devon stretched as Keisha's alarm went off next to him, rolling over to study her beautiful face. He was reluctant to wake her, knowing he'd kept her up last night, but he knew how important her job was to her. He nuzzled into her neck, nipping her skin lightly.

"Up, mamas," he whispered into her ear.

She sighed and rolled over, cuddling into him. "Just a few more minutes."

He tightened his hold on her. "You could stay home all day with me," he coaxed.

She snorted, giving him her answer to that. He chuckled and kissed the top of her head, then let her lay in silence until her alarm went off again. This time, she groaned. He separated their bodies and got out of her bed, heading into the bathroom to start the shower for her.

An hour later, after getting her on the road, he was on his way to his own meeting. He pulled up to the Knights' department store, nodding in approval at what his friend had built. But then, he didn't expect anything less from Mason. He'd always been focused and steady.

Following the instructions Julian had given him to get to his offices on the upper floor of the building, Devon entered the elevator code. Moments later, he got off, looking around at his friend's setup. It was dope. He looked up as Deena came out of her mate's office. She smiled at him warmly. He didn't know her as well as his brother did, but he would always have a soft spot for those who grew up with them and in the struggle the way they had.

"Welcome home, Devon," she told him.

He pulled her into a hug. "Look at you, all grown up."

"A whole adult out here." She laughed and stepped back, rubbing her pregnant stomach. "I'm sure Declan is excited. You can go right in, Junior said he was waiting for you."

"Congratulations," he told her before heading to his friend's office.

Julian stood as he came in, rounding his desk. He dapped him up and pulled him into a half-hug. Devon plopped into the chair in front of the desk, getting comfortable.

"Been enjoying your time out?" Julian asked as he settled back into his own chair.

"Making moves, enjoying the sun on my face," he told his friend. "Congratulations on the baby. I'm 'bout to buy a drum set for my niece or nephew right now."

"Man, go to hell." Julian cackled. "I need to go see this house Declan picked. What brings you to see me?"

"Since I've been out, my mind has been on how I ended up in prison. Leland was killed right after, and the shit don't feel like a coincidence," Devon explained.

Julian frowned. "Senior always said he thought you were set up. But the 'how' was the sticking point." He studied Devon. "You sure you want to go down this rabbit hole?"

"If I got somebody out to get me, I want to know. I can't spend the rest of my life looking over my shoulder." Especially not with his mate. He didn't want that life for them. His phone rang; it was his brother. He ignored it. He could call Declan back once he left Julian's office.

"I talked to Tangie the other night to find out who the car we were riding in belonged to. She told me it was Marcus Cartwright's."

"Councilman Cartwright's son?" Julian looked up at him in surprise. "That's who she had the baby by?"

Devon nodded. "She says the drugs were planted, that Marcus wasn't really into that kind of thing. But my question is how they would've ever met in the first place." He'd wanted to ask her that, but something had held him back. "Could it have been planted to get Marcus thrown in jail?"

Julian whistled. "On some real shit, that's exactly how Cyrus moves. I need to call Unc and give him a heads up. Marcus was in college when his father's seat was taken. Councilman Crespo was the only reason Cyrus didn't kill him when he came back into town."

"So, you think Cyrus could've been trying to get rid of him by putting him in jail versus killing him?"

Julian shrugged. "Shit, he ended up killing the kid anyways, not too long after Leland died."

Devon frowned because he didn't know the details of Marcus's death. He just knew that Tangie had been torn up over it.

"I was just caught in the crossfire?" But then he thought about the drive-by and the car that was after him the other day. He never ignored his instincts, and they were screaming that someone was actively plotting on him. "Declan hasn't made any moves toward his position yet. So, why would Cyrus be after me now?"

"You think he's still after you?" Julian leaned back in his chair.

"My position in the streets ain't really change even with the prison sentence. Maybe I'm in the way." He frowned as his phone rang again. He silenced it and continued with Julian. "Too many coincidences happening. A drive-by within days of me being back. The other night when I left Tangie's, I was followed, and I'm pretty sure they were coming after me. I got saved by a family in a minivan."

Julian cursed. "What?"

"Yeah, shit was finna go down." Devon shook his head.

"You a little too nonchalant about this," Julian said, his face a thundercloud.

"Man, you know how I used to live. This ain't shit. If it wasn't for Declan and Keisha, I would've been on the hunt." His phone rang again. His brother was persistent; clearly, something was wrong. "Yeah, Dec?"

"Yo, where you at?" Declan's voice was frantic.

"Chilling with Julian at his office."

Declan blew out a relieved breath. "Ok. Ok. That's good."

"What happened?" He sat forward.

"Someone shot up a Charger across the tracks. I thought..." His brother sighed.

"Dec, I'm safe. I'm on the South side, so whatever's going on ain't got shit to do with me."

"You sure about that?" his brother asked.

He opened his mouth to answer but thought about what he'd just told Julian. Could someone still be after him? If he counted this incident as being aimed at him, then that would make three separate times someone had come after him.

Shit.

"I'll hit you back when I'm done here."

"Go home after this, Dev," his brother ordered.

"I'ma let you make it because I can feel your stress, but I'm grown, little brother."

Declan growled. "You think it's a coincidence that—"

He cut him off. "I'll handle it, Dec."

His brother disconnected the call without saying anything, which let him know how pissed he was. Devon ran his hand across his face and groaned. What the fuck was going on?

"What was that?" Julian asked, pulling his attention.

"Declan said there was a shooting across the tracks."

Julian's eyes narrowed. "Why was he worried for you?"

"It was a Charger." Devon sucked his teeth because he was irritated. He wanted to get out of prison and help his brother before chilling on all this shit.

"Dev..." Julian started.

Devon sighed. "Yeah, I know, man. Suggestions?"

"Only thing I can think is for Declan to challenge him now. If Cyrus aiming at you, then he'll step up the threats, but once the Motsi know that Declan's coming after the seat, he'll be under more scrutiny."

"I got a couple of moves to put in place before Declan does that. I want to make sure he's covered. I ain't worried about me."

He went through the list of stuff he wanted to do. First up was making sure Declan had the shooters he needed. It was going to piss his brother off, but he needed to go back across the tracks. The sooner he turned his connects over, the sooner they could be done with that part.

"You ain't worried about you, but you have a mate to consider now," Julian reminded him.

It paused his steps. Keisha wanted him out, and this would guarantee it. But...he didn't think she would like the way he was going about it. He shook his head.

"I'll handle it," was his reply.

He prayed that he could do it without too much trouble.

15...

Every year, Silas Knight put on a fundraiser for various charities in the city. It was his way of showing Eastfield that he was working for all shifters and not just the feline ones. This year, it was for the Little Leagues set up around the city. It would cover the costs for setting up the teams and all the traveling they would need to do. It had been Julissa's idea, and Keisha was honestly excited about it.

Well, she had been an hour ago.

She'd left Devon's house this morning, rushing into work and ignoring his hints that he was ready for her to move in. It felt too soon. Her wolf was sinking fast, and it wasn't giving her time to come to grips with the fact that Devon would be her mate — and would be plunging them into the Motsi.

Plus, her cousins were ringing down her line to ask her about a shooting that had happened yesterday. Despite the fact that she'd fussed at them about calling her at work with bad news, Keisha had been bombarded with messages all morning. Rumor had it that Devon was involved, but he'd not said anything to her last night when she was at his house. Couple that with the fact that she was already having women in her face about him and she was over it. Well, to be fair, it was only one woman, but still.

It was the principle.

She'd joked with him that he would have her fighting women all over town, but she didn't want that to be her life. She was all discombobulated, her mind in shambles as she pulled up to the gate of the

Knights' family home. Taking deep breaths, she worked to push away her bad mood.

She swallowed down her irritation and fixed her face as Adina Knight came out her front door. Keisha parked in the circular driveway and got out, grabbing all the materials the party planner had asked for. She was supposed to meet her here, along with Mila, Silas's wife, so they could get all the last-minute details together.

"Hi, Keisha," Adina greeted, pulling her into a hug.

She rubbed her cheek along the older woman's in greeting, smiling as the powerful animal within Adina Knight rushed to assert its place.

"Good afternoon, Mrs. Knight."

They both turned as another car pulled into the compound.

"Go on inside, Iris is in the kitchen," Adina told her.

Nodding, Keisha headed into the elegant home. She'd been here several times over the years she'd worked for Silas, so she knew her way around. The kitchen was massive and pristine. Iris Campbell was Adina Knight's cousin, but she worked for them, so Keisha never knew quite what to call her. Iris was slicing fruit at the counter, adding to the rest of the food spread across the kitchen island.

"Ms. Iris," she greeted the woman. "How are you?"

"Good, baby. You want some?" Iris didn't give Keisha any time to answer, simply setting a plate in front of her as she took a seat at one of the high-backed stools.

She knew telling the woman no would be useless, so she speared a piece of watermelon with her fork.

"What's wrong?" Ms. Iris was studying her as she continued to arrange fruit on a tray.

Keisha's eyes widened at the woman's intuitiveness. "What do you mean?"

Ms. Iris inhaled deeply before a smile broke out across her face. "Oooh! Adina, get in here, girl!" she called out, turning around to the sink to wash her hands.

Adina rushed in, her grandson in her arms and Mila on her tail. "What happened?"

Keisha stood and greeted Mila, rubbing a finger across Carter's cute face. He was his father's spitting image.

"You must not have been paying attention," Iris said. She waved her hand under her own nose.

Adina frowned but leaned over and sniffed at Keisha. She barked out a laugh. "Well, now this is interesting."

Keisha bit her lip, intending to stay silent, but the women weren't having it.

Mila, not one to be left out, inhaled and frowned. "I don't get it."

Adina waved off her daughter-in-law. "You're still learning. Keisha's scent has changed. It's melded with one Iris and I are very familiar with."

Iris cackled. "If she can keep Silas in line, it should be fairly easy for her to keep Devon's hardheaded ass out of trouble."

"Wait, what?" It was Keisha frowning this time.

Adina snickered. "That boy was a handful and a half."

Keisha sighed. "He still is," she muttered.

"You want some tips?" Adina asked, her eyes sparkling.

"Bust his tail over the head a couple of times," Iris said, and they both busted out laughing.

Adina put a hand on her arm. "Soft," she told her. "Them boys have had to scrounge and fight for everything they have. They're rough, mama. Give him softness."

"You gotta go old-school with that one," Iris suggested. "Soften yourself for him, let him take control. It's all him and his brother know."

She didn't even know how to do that. Her father had treated her like a princess and losing him had been a shocking dose of reality. Keisha could admit that she'd hardened herself and her heart to cope. Could she let down those walls for Devon?

"He's so damn…dominant and bossy," Keisha whined.

Mila laughed next to her. "Girl! Ain't it aggravating?"

"Yes!" she exhaled, happy someone else understood.

Iris sucked her teeth at them both and shook her head. "Y'all need to learn finesse. It's all 'yes, love,' 'whatever you say, love,' and then gently guide them into what's right. Ain't nobody got time for all that arguing."

"You sound like my mama," Keisha grumbled. The women laughed, but she was dead serious. "Mama's spoiling and mothering him, talking 'bout '*that's a man, Keisha,*'" she mocked.

Iris fell out, laughing. "Let that man cut the grass and build you a shed and watch he treat you like gold."

Keisha opened her mouth to give them her independent speech, but Iris held up her hand.

"I'ma stop you right there, girlboss. Give him your boundaries and meet him where he's at. Being soft requires a shit ton of trust. Listen to your animal and let Devon show you that he can take care of you."

"Set your boundaries from now and communicate. Hell, you do it every day with Silas. Just use the same tactics," Adina told her.

She nodded, happy she'd opened up to the women. "Thank you."

"Of course, love." Adina squeezed her hand. "I'm excited for you."

Keisha juggled the bags in her hand, growling as her phone rang again. Devon had been calling her for the last hour. She hadn't felt like fussing with him while she was grocery shopping, so she'd texted him that she'd call later. She guessed Devon decided that enough time had passed.

"Yes, Devon?" she finally answered after dropping the bags onto her kitchen counter.

"Why you ignoring me, Key? I don't like that shit."

Her wolf moved through her body at his agitated tone. She could only sigh at the easy animal. Remembering why she was irritated with him, she straightened her posture.

"I heard you were in another shooting across the tracks," she told him.

"I don't know who gave you that information, but it ain't have shit to do with me." He sighed. "How you mad at me about some shit without talking to me?"

"You're supposed to be getting out, Devon," she said, exasperated.

"And I am, Key. I wasn't even there."

"So why I keep getting calls about it?"

"How the fuck I'm 'posed to know that, love?" he growled.

"It's too much, Devon. Gotta deal with rumors, gotta fight bitches in the street, when does it end?"

"I'm not trying to fight with you," he insisted.

"You always say you don't want to fight and yet here we are," she snapped.

"I been locked in a cage with shifters who ain't got nothing to lose. I didn't come out of prison to be in the same shit, love." His voice was firm, the dominance in it making her wolf fold. "I don't break my word, Key. If I say I'm finna do some shit, then that's what it is. I'm getting out. I'm not trying to put you through it, I swear."

Her pulse stuttered and her breath caught. "Devon," she managed in a whisper.

"Open the door, Key," he ordered.

She swallowed the lump in her throat and did as he demanded. He was on the other side, fine as hell, his wolf flashing in his eyes. God, how was she supposed to deny this man anything? He entered and closed the door behind him, locking it. Before she could walk away, he gripped her arm, pulling her into his chest. He cupped her chin and brought her face closer to his.

"I been fighting since I slid into this world, Key. I'm not on that shit no more. I want peace, goddammit, and if that means I gotta be around here on some simp shit, then that's just what it is. That don't mean you 'bout to have me ripping and running after your ass."

She heard the warning, knowing his patience was but so long. He nuzzled into her neck, and she sighed as her body relaxed under his touch. Her wolf was gone for him, and only Keisha was keeping the animal from getting what it wanted.

She nodded.

"I missed you today," he whispered against her lips.

"I missed you too," she admitted.

She knew she was in love with him, but the part of her that worried he would end up like her father was holding her back. He lifted her as she wrapped her arms around his neck.

"I gotta put away my groceries," she complained halfheartedly.

He ignored her, kissing her deeply and carrying her into her bedroom.

16...

The coincidences were stacking up, and Devon knew that he had stumbled onto some bit of truth. It was the only reason he could think for someone to be actively targeting him. He changed lanes and cursed when the same car from the other night was tailing him again. This time, it wasn't full, just a single driver.

He liked those odds.

He was supposed to be meeting Drew so they could discuss the turnover. Devon had several warehouses he used to operate out of and had scheduled the meeting in the one at the furthest end of the district. It was serendipitous, really.

Leading the driver across the tracks, he knew a place where he could go for some semblance of privacy. Turning into the warehouse district, he pulled up to a stop sign, knowing the driver wouldn't be able to resist. He pulled his pistol from the center console and waited, popping his trunk. Sure enough, the driver pulled beside him. Devon didn't give the male any time, firing into his car as the driver lifted his own tool. He shattered the passenger window and shot again, keeping the wound non-lethal.

Jumping out of his Charger, he rounded the front of the lowrider the other male was driving. He smashed the window and aimed. "Out the fucking car."

"Fuck you," he spat.

Devon chuckled. "Oh, it's fuck me, huh?"

He reached in and dragged the man through the shattered glass, smiling as he screamed. Devon wasted no time, making sure the male was scraping against the concrete as he dragged him to his Charger. Tossing him in the trunk, he slammed it shut. He turned around and sent two shots into the engine block of the lowrider, making sure it would be there when he sent some people to come get it.

Jumping back into the driver's seat, he called Drew, making his way through the narrow streets to the warehouse where their meeting was being held.

"What up?" Drew answered.

"Got some shit I need you to help me get out of the car."

"The fuck I look like? Your valet?"

Devon sucked his teeth. "Bitch, spell valet. Bring your ass, I'm outside." He tucked his phone in his back pocket and got out the car.

Drew swaggered up to him just as he was opening the trunk. The dude's breathing was labored, and he could see patches of fur where the male's animal had been trying to shift in order to heal him. But Devon packed nothing but silver, so the wolf was fighting through the poison.

"Who the fuck is this?" Drew's eyebrows were bunched as he peered into the trunk.

Devon shrugged. "We'll find out soon enough, won't we?"

Drew waved over some of the soldiers guarding the warehouse. They came and snatched the man out of Devon's trunk and carried him to the building. They paused at the door, waiting on Drew to type in the code to open it. The fact that it was locked told Devon that his friend was either actively stashing work or money.

His eyes skimmed the interior, seeing drugs lined up on metal shelves along the wall. There were a couple other males standing at the railing of the second floor, overseeing the workers bagging drugs at two tables toward the end of the warehouse. He followed Drew as his men carried the cursing male up the stairs and to a separate large, empty room off to the right. Devon was familiar with it being as he'd used it as storage once upon a time. He would've never had drugs down on the first floor where anyone could see if the door opened the right way.

He would warn Drew about it before he left.

There was only a single wooden table with several empty money counters on it and aluminum chairs. Devon watched dispassionately while they tied him to a chair in the sparsely furnished room.

Once the male was tied, Devon moved closer. "Who sent you after me?"

His head was hanging, low, his pain easy to read. It took him a minute, but the male raised his head, his eyes flashing between the amber of his animal and the dark brown of his human form.

"I ain't saying shit," he was finally able to get out.

Devon pressed his gun into the wound on his shoulder. The man yelled out.

"I'm not asking you again."

"You gon' kill me anyway," the man answered.

"Eventually," Devon replied honestly. "There's a lot of shit in between, though."

The male hissed in pain, his eyes darting all over the warehouse before smirking. "Shit done changed since you been in. People ain't the same."

Devon cocked back and hit him in the head with his pistol, and the male coughed and groaned.

"You trusting—"

Devon flinched at the blast of the gun. The deafening bang of it ricocheted off the walls of the room and he tightened his finger on his trigger reflexively. Blood splattered across his chest and clothes. He cursed and turned to his friend in time to watch Drew lower his .45.

"Man, what the fuck?"

His ears were ringing, and Devon fought with his instinct to up his shit and bust his friend over the head. The old him would have. He reminded himself that he was trying to change. Still, his wolf rumbled his chest, the pads of his fingers aching with the press of his claws ready to descend.

"He wasn't finna say shit, and we got shit to do today," Drew explained.

Devon stepped back from the dead body. "I wasn't finished questioning him."

Drew shrugged and reached into the male's pocket. "I can find out what we need without him," he said, holding up his wallet.

Devon sucked his teeth and pulled out his ringing phone. It was Keisha's mom. "Hey, ma."

"I'm sorry to bother you. Are you busy?" she asked.

He tucked his gun into the back of his pants. "Not if you need something."

She simpered. "Keisha hates when I go to the shelter alone and my sister can't come with me today."

"Okay. When you need me?"

"Now, if you're available."

"I can be there in like thirty." He looked down at the splatter over his shirt. "No, make that closer to an hour. I need to go home and change cars so you'll be more comfortable."

It wasn't exactly a lie. Drew cursed next to him.

"Okay, I can wait. Thank you."

"I got you, ma." He hung up and gave his friend a questioning look.

"I thought we were supposed to be going through this turnover shit. We need to set it up so I can meet your plug." Drew chuckled. "You ain't even mated yet and she got you running around."

"It is what it is," Devon said, dismissing his friend. "I'll get up with you."

He left the warehouse and headed home. After a shower, he called Rocco to send someone to come clean out his car. Rock didn't ask any questions. Devon made it to Ms. Patrice's house within the allotted hour, knocking on her door.

She answered with a smile, handing him a huge duffel bag. She was in scrubs with dancing candy all over them. Her hair was pulled back into a ponytail and she looked adorable. His mate was gonna be fine as hell as she aged if Ms. Patrice was anything to go by.

He nuzzled the top of her head in greeting. "Where we headed?"

"I don't know if Keisha told you, but since I retired, I help some of the local shelters with medical issues. There's a doctor that comes in once a month, and in between, I take care of the small stuff."

Devon nodded because she had talked to him about it. "I think that's dope, ma."

She smiled as he led her to his Range and helped her in. They made idle chit-chat until they pulled up to a building he was familiar with. He and his brother had spent a couple of months in the care home.

Ms. Patrice turned to him. "How did you and your brother end up in a group home on the South side?"

He wiped a hand across his face, the memories of those tumultuous years going through his mind. "This one didn't have the space to keep us both. It worked out better in the end," he assured her, thinking about the friends he'd made in that group home.

She hummed. "Yeah, the funds aren't where they need to be still. Councilman Booth isn't investing in people like he should be."

Devon understood what she meant and knew that Declan would be different, better than Cyrus. They spent a couple of hours there and then were back on the road to the next place. The homeless shelter they pulled into next was bustling and damn near busting out of the seams. He helped Ms. Patrice set up her first aid station and settled back, watching over her as she worked.

He took in the center, noting how many of the residents were kids with their parents or fresh out of the foster system. He made a mental note to talk to Rock about the housing situation he'd set up. There needed to be something for those kids who had aged out of the system but weren't quite ready to be on their own. It had been him once upon a time, and he knew that panicked feeling well.

By the time Ms. Patrice was done at the homeless shelter, he had a bunch of ideas. It really brought home how much work he and Declan would have to do to turn the West side around.

Before he could start the car, Ms. Patrice grabbed his wrist. He gave her his attention, noting her serious expression.

"Most of the time, the people on the bottom pay for the decisions of those at the top. This place, the others… It's all a result of someone taking more than their fair share."

He studied her face, understanding what she was trying to convey. "My brother's a good man. We grew up in this, ma. We both understand what's at stake."

She nodded, satisfied with his answer. Smiling softly, Patrice cupped his cheek. "I love that you call me mama. Maybe it will light a fire under my daughter's ass."

The switch in subject had him barking out a laugh.

"That girl loves her job, so we probably ain't gonna get a baby anytime soon," she lamented.

He laughed harder. "I gotta go on her time, mama."

Once again, he'd enjoyed his time with her mother. He helped her cook, and they talked as though she'd actually birthed him. It soothed his wolf. By the time he was done, he had plates for him and his mate. He decided to pull up on her versus trying to convince her to come out to his house. They'd been working on their mating for close to a month, and so far, he'd been unsuccessful in convincing her to move in with him.

Her car was not in its spot when he arrived. He drummed his fingers on the steering wheel and debated his next move. He could probably break in. Devon nodded, deciding that's what he would do. He called her first to see how close she was to coming home. It was barely after five, so she could possibly be nearly here.

"I'm working, babe." Was her tired greeting.

"You work too much, mamas," was his answer to that.

"I love my job," she grumbled.

He got out of his truck, headed for her front door. "Still don't change the facts, shawty." He grunted as he made easy work of her lock, which really pissed him off. "What time you headed home?"

She sighed. "I'm finishing up now. But I'm headed to my place."

Devon sucked his teeth but decided arguing with her about that could wait since he was currently in her apartment.

"I ain't even say nothing, Key."

"I'll call you when I get home," she said softly.

"A'ight, mamas." He could hear the exhaustion in her voice, so he hung up. He shook his head and let it go. She would learn one way or the other.

17...

There was a moment when Keisha debated driving to Devon's house instead of her own. He'd probably cooked and so she wouldn't have to. That was appealing, but mostly, she missed him. Even when she'd been upset with him earlier, she still wanted to see him. She thought about Ms. Adina's words. Would she be able to keep Devon out of trouble? From the phone calls and texts she received, it was unlikely.

Sighing, she kept going on the highway toward her house, passing the exit that would take her to his. She needed to go home. Arguing with her mate was not on her agenda tonight. She groaned as her phone rang and her mother's name appeared on the car screen. She'd talked to Patrice on her lunch, so two calls in a day probably meant she needed something.

"Hey, mama."

"You sound tired, baby. I thought once your boss mated, you two would get somewhere and sit down."

Keisha snorted. For the most part that was true, but long hours were the normal once the session was over and it was time to enact most the legislature they'd managed to get passed.

"I talked to you earlier, lady. Did you need something?"

"No, I just called to see if you were home and to chat. That's it," Patrice answered.

"Oh!" She couldn't help the surprise in her voice.

"Excuse your nerve," her mother chuckled. "I don't just call to ask you for stuff."

"I know, mama."

"And besides, my son done been over here and helped me out today."

Her eyebrows winged high as she turned into her neighborhood. "Devon?"

"Yep." Patrice's voice was smug. "I just sent my baby home with a plate a few hours ago."

"Dang, he your baby now?"

Patrice chuckled. "Not you jealous. I sent something for you too, that's why I was calling. You ain't make it home yet?"

"Pulling up now," she said absently, recognizing Devon's vehicle.

"Ok. Well, I won't keep you. Dinner Sunday?"

"Yes, ma'am," she agreed.

"I love you."

"Love you too," she murmured.

Devon opened her front door and leaned against the jamb, his eyes ever watchful. He looked comfortable in a black t-shirt and matching shorts.

She hadn't given him a key, but she didn't even have to wonder how he got in. The fact that he'd been able to do so would more than likely be his main point when he brought it up later — because he would. Keisha dragged her tired body out of the car.

Devon took her briefcase and kissed her forehead. Tears clogged her throat. She hadn't realized how it would feel to come home to him. She was tired and probably was taking on too much, but it was the only way she knew how to move. She'd been on go from the moment she graduated from college and had yet to let up.

Devon lifted her chin. "You look overwhelmed. What's the matter, baby?"

She took a deep, shuddering breath. "Nothing, I just— I don't have time or headspace for company, but I don't want you to go."

He pulled her in tighter, rubbing her back and not saying anything. Her body melted into his and her wolf preened under his attention. His chest rumbled with a growl, his animal acknowledging hers. She nuzzled into his chest, content to spend the rest of the evening this way. The spicy scent of his cologne warmed her, but then the scents of dinner intruded. Added to that was the smell of cleaning products.

She lifted her head and looked around in awe.

Keisha knew for a fact there had been chip bags and books scattered across her glass coffee table. The pillows and throw blanket on her small sectional were placed neatly. She could even see the lines where he'd vacuumed the throw rug over her wood floor. She glanced at her kitchen and saw the dishes she'd left in the drying rack put away. All the mail that had been chucked on the counter surface was gone too.

She turned back to him with wide eyes. "You cleaned?"

"You messy as hell, shawty, but I wouldn't want to clean either if I kept up the hours you do. Go change, mama sent food over. I'm warming yours as we speak." Devon stepped back from her.

She wanted to drop to her knees and thank him properly. It must have shown in her eyes as he growled and moved nearer. The full moon was close, wreaking havoc on her body because going from emotional to demon time that quickly was wild.

"A'ight now, my baby, you trying to start some shit, and I'm trying to take care of my mate."

Keisha closed the distance between them and hugged him tight. "Thank you," she whispered.

"Anything for you, love." Lifting her chin, Devon dropped two soft kisses. "Go," he ordered softly, patting her ass.

That was an easy enough direction to follow, so she headed to her bathroom, washing her face and hands and changing. By the time she returned, he had their food put on the table. She hugged his back as he opened wine.

"I didn't think I would like this fruity shit, but you got the good stuff," he murmured.

Taking the proffered glass, Keisha went up on her toes and offered him her lips for a kiss. He deepened it, and the moan she released came from her toes.

"Sit and eat, mamas," he ordered, walking her back to her chair.

She smiled as they ate in a companiable silence. Any other person would be fighting to fill the quiet, but Devon didn't. It seemed he was content to just be with her. That was appealing in every way. It was one of the little things that showed Keisha they were compatible, despite the way she fought him.

"Mama said you went by today?"

He nodded. "I helped her at the shelters."

She'd forgotten that was today. "She usually does it with my aunt."

"Auntie May was busy today."

Keisha chuckled. "You just claiming all my family."

He smiled, and her stomach did a slow tumble as goosebumps rose all over her skin. God, the man was just...

She sighed and took a deep gulp of her wine. "Thank you for that."

"Quit playing with me, shawty. I done told you I take care of what's mine."

She tipped her glass to him, conceding that. She sighed as her body finally relaxed, the wine and his presence loosening her tight muscles. That didn't last long, though, his next order immediately erasing the relaxed feeling.

"You need to move in with me, Key," he fussed.

She sighed. "Devon, we just started dating."

He scoffed. "Dating? We're mates, love, which means you're stalling."

"I'm not, I just..." she left off, and he chuckled.

"Just what I said. Your apartment isn't safe enough, anyway."

Keisha snorted because she knew that was coming. "Only because you and your brother are stirring up shit. Otherwise, nobody would even be checking for me."

"Yeah, ok."

She growled. "I'm too tired to deal with this shit tonight."

"Tone, Key," he told her, and she sighed.

"Sorry," she murmured.

He reached across the table and grabbed her hand, bringing it up to his lips, kissing her skin gently. "If you were at my place, I could be taking some of that pressure off you."

"Devon," she said softly.

"I'm just saying, shawty. You ain't gotta handle all this shit alone. I'm here now, and it's only so long I'ma wait on you to start trusting me before I take some decisions out of your hands."

She could only nod, understanding the warning.

Keisha's phone rang for the fourth time this morning, and once again, she ignored it. She was in Silas's office going over some research and she didn't have the head space to deal with her persistent mate. She'd left Devon at her place, rushing out to avoid picking up their argument from last night. She made a mental note to call Lucky when she got off today because she needed some advice. But now that she thought about it, her cousin would give her the same advice Patrice had offered.

Why was she fighting this man so hard?

During her drive to work this morning, she'd mostly worked out that he reminded her so much of her father. She wasn't built like Patrice, so putting up with the shit that came with the streets wasn't in her. If it was just the danger, she didn't think she'd have any issues with that, but the women, the constant gossip fodder that came with being a hood legend? Yeah, she wasn't built for that because the way her mouth was set up, she didn't put up with a lot of shit from people.

She growled as her phone rang again. This time, she put it on silent. When she looked up, Silas and Rock were both staring at her. The three of them were in Silas's office working. Well, Rocco was just in there in his capacity as security, but still.

"Better answer it before he bring his big ass into this office after you," Silas warned casually as he typed on his tablet.

She sucked her teeth knowing full damn well they wouldn't let his ass in the building.

Silas snickered. "What's the matter?"

"He thinks he's somebody's damn daddy." She didn't bring up the actual argument because she feared both men would be on Devon's side.

Her boss laughed outright.

"If you wanted someone you can run over, should've told your wolf to choose one of these soft ass pussies around this building," Rocco commented.

She barely restrained from rolling her eyes. "I do not want someone I can run over," she protested." Her wolf would never accept someone less dominant than them, unfortunately.

"Liar," Silas taunted. "It's close to the full moon. You better quit playing with that man."

She shuddered because she should've realized that was why her own wolf was so snappy. Silas's personal phone rang, and instead of answering it, he simply passed it to Keisha. Her eyes widened.

"What?" she growled into the phone.

"Aye, you gon' get enough of that attitude around me."

"I'm working, Devon."

"You always working. What you want for lunch?"

She opened her mouth but then closed it because that wasn't what she was expecting. "I…" She looked at Silas. "I have plans for lunch," she lied.

Both Silas and Rocco snickered.

"A'ight, bet."

That was all Devon said before hanging up. She passed the phone back to Silas and breathed a sigh of relief. The room was silent, but she knew both of these men like the back of her hand.

"What?"

"I ain't even say anything," Silas said.

She sighed in resignation. "Just spit it out."

"He finna come down here and show his ass," he warned her.

Her back straightened in shock. "He wouldn't."

Rocco snorted. "The hell he won't."

"They won't let him in." She looked between the two men for confirmation.

"Pops already put him and his brother on the approved visitor list."

"What? When? Oh, God," she whispered. She whipped out her phone and tried to call him, but it went straight to voicemail. She frowned. "He's ignoring me," she muttered.

Silas checked his watch. "What's on the schedule for the rest of the morning?"

"You have two conference calls," she said absently.

"Let's go over them right now, just in case something comes up." He cut eyes at Rocco, who laughed and shook his head, going back to whatever he was doing on his laptop.

Keisha tried Devon twice more, but he didn't answer. She sighed and went to work.

18...

Devon pulled up to the building and studied it. The imposing structure was made of mostly glass in the front. Shaped like a rhombus, it was a combination of black stone and dark woods. He knew most of the offices were underground, with most of what was visible only housing the public areas. It was a big fucking deal, and his brother would soon be in the thick of this shit.

He still wasn't sure how he felt about it, but he was rocking with his brother no matter what happened. He pulled the lunch he'd made for Keisha out of the passenger seat and shook his head. That stubborn ass girl wouldn't let him take care of her. It was driving his wolf up the wall. It didn't help that the full moon was tonight. He was forcing the animal down even as he locked his heat in his glove compartment and got out the car.

Security eyed him hard as they checked him in. If they knew how close he was to snapping, they would move differently. There were two men at the door, but as he entered the building, two more materialized out of nowhere. Devon's eyes darted across the lobby, and he spotted a couple of wolves in suits watching him. He smiled, lowering his canines. It would seem them motherfuckers knew who he was already. One of them pulled out a phone, probably reporting directly to Councilman Booth. He narrowed his eyes as one of the guards moved to search him.

"Watch the fucking hands," he growled.

The lion shifter snarled but backed off. "Get a badge at the desk."

"Pussy," Devon grumbled, swaggering into the building.

The receptionist found his name easy enough, sliding a visitor's badge toward him.

"Which way is Silas Knight's office?"

"I can take you there," a sweet voice said from behind him.

He looked down at the bear female. She wore a green pencil skirt with a white blouse tucked into it. Shit looked elegant, everything about her screaming money. She smiled, holding out her hand.

"I'm Julissa, Rocco's mate. You're Devon, right?"

He nodded, smiling at the beautiful sow. He shook her proffered hand. "Nice to meet you, shawty."

"Nice to finally meet you. PD has told me a lot about you and your brother."

He walked beside Julissa, silencing his phone as it rang again. His mate was trying to get in touch with him, which meant Silas had warned her that he was the type to pull up. He didn't do a lot of back and forth, but his mate would soon find that out. Julissa chatted next to him, and Devon could see why the bear loved her. She was sweet, that much was obvious; it was just funny how completely opposite she was to her mate.

"Here we are," she said, using a key card to open the door to the offices, which was a good thing because in his mood, he would've just torn the door down. Before he could get in good, Keisha came rushing down the hallway.

"What are you doing here?" She grabbed his hand and pulled him into a conference room across the hall from their offices, locking the door behind her.

"What's wrong with you?" he asked, lifting her chin.

"There's nothing wrong."

He smelled the astringent scent of her lies. "What I told you about lying to me?"

"You are not my damn daddy, Devon."

He set her lunch on the table and growled. See, his mate was trying him, and that shit was finna stop. Slipping his hand around her throat, he collared her lightly, backing her against the wall. Her breath caught. He slid his claws down and trailed them up Keisha's thighs. She'd left her house this morning in a midnight blue wrap dress made of the softest cashmere. Pushing the material aside, he skated his fingers across the seam of her panties.

"This little attitude shit ain't working for me, lil mama."

He ripped her underwear away and pulled his claws back. He glided a finger across her pussy, finding her wet and scorching to the touch.

"Devon," she whispered. "We can't."

He kept her hemmed by her neck, shoving two fingers into her clenching sex. He curled them to press on her g-spot and watched her eyes roll back into her head.

"I'm not trying to be your daddy. I'm trying to take care of your hardheaded ass." Her back arched and her wolf lit her eyes. "You on yo' independent shit, and I fucks with that, Keisha, but you. Are. Mine." He thrust into her, punctuating his words. "That means mine to take care of, mine to love, and mine to protect."

He bit her ear and sucked it into his mouth, his fingers pumping in and out of her. She whimpered and his dick bricked up, pushing against his zipper.

"You do not ignore me when I'm trying to reach you, understand?" He pressed against her spot again, sucking on her neck.

She nodded.

"Words," he ordered.

She whimpered as her pussy squeezed down on his fingers.

"Yes."

"You got some shit on your chest, you tell me and we talk about it. None of this attitude shit, hear?"

She closed her mouth and tucked her lips, rubbing her sex against his palm. He squeezed her neck and her eyes flew open. He kissed her, devouring her mouth, their tongues dueling. He couldn't help it. He battled with his animal for control, understanding his wolf's obsession with their mate. Every facet of Keisha consumed him. She preoccupied his thoughts when they were apart.

Her mewls of pleasure were soothing his wolf and taking the edge off of his bad mood. He pulled back, sliding his fingers until he was nearly out of her pussy.

"No," she whispered. "Please."

"We done with this attitude shit?" He rubbed his head along her hair, assuaging his animal's need to reassure her wolf.

"Devon," she whimpered, arching her hips to try and push his fingers back in.

Devon pulled them out all the way, but then he pinched on her clit, and she gasped. "We done, shawty, or should I just leave?"

Her little hardheaded ass turned her head. He squeezed her throat a little tighter and felt her stomach contract. She tried to close her legs so she could squelch the fire between them.

"Aht-aht," he said, pushing his thigh between her legs, careful to keep it from where she wanted.

"Fuck," she cursed.

Devon leaned over her neck and nipped her skin. "Answer me, Keisha. What you wanna do? I can send you back to your office with lunch and an amazing orgasm, or I can send you back with lunch horny than a motherfucker with that same ass attitude. What's the move?"

"Orgasm," she whispered, her lip poked out, pouting.

God, he found that sexy as fuck. He kissed her softly, sliding his finger across her clit.

"I'm not one of these bitch ass shifters around here. I already told you I'm not 'bout to let you run me. But I'm also not trying to dim your light, love. I'm just asking for you to let me in your life. Is that unreasonable?"

She shook her head, her eyes wet with emotion. He kissed her gently, pushing his fingers into her needy pussy. He finger-fucked her, never releasing her mouth. He swallowed her whimpers as she came, her body tightening. Her heartbeat was racing in her chest and his wolf was begging him to mark her, if only temporarily. He nipped her bottom lip as her body went limp. She released a shaky breath, the lust slowly clearing from her gaze as she seemed to remember where they were.

"Devon," she sighed softly. "I can't be doing this at work."

"That's your fault. If you would've answered my calls, I wouldn't have had to come down here and give you some act right."

"My God," she whispered, hiding her smile.

He helped her fix her clothes and backed away. She gave him soft eyes and his heart clenched. She lifted her chin and gave him her neck, and Devon's wolf bucked in satisfaction.

"I'm sorry for my attitude."

He slid his cheek against her neck, accepting her submission to him. He wrapped his arms around his mate. She returned his hug.

"I'll communicate better."

"You got a college degree, you better."

She sucked her teeth. "Now, see…"

He smiled and gripped her chin, dropping a gentle kiss to her lips. "I'm fucking with you, baby."

She rolled her eyes. "Thank you for lunch."

"Of course. You working late?"

She shook her head.

"So then, where will you be after work?" he tested.

She sighed. "At your house."

"See how easy that was, my baby?" He kissed her and opened the door for her. "Have a good day."

He had his own shit to do, and he already knew Drew was finna cuss him out behind being late, but his wolf was not having all the tension between him and their mate. He threw up a head nod to Rock and headed back out of the building.

Devon leaned against the banister of his back porch, staring past his pool to the ocean waves beyond. Though nightfall was hours away, he could feel the call of the moon. Wolves were more susceptible to it than the other shifters, even though this town as a whole tended to revel in it. Even now, he watched people gather at the beach to await the sun's descent.

His wolf was restless, sending goosebumps in its wake as it paced his body. If he shifted now, he wasn't sure what the wolf would do. So, instead of doing what the animal wanted, he'd cleaned his house. That was done, but now he waited on his mate to get home.

Keisha was probably being affected by it, but that fucking stubborn woman was most likely ignoring the pull of the moon. It was one of the reasons he'd insisted she come out to his house tonight. He didn't know what she did during the full moon prior to him, but he would be the only person to sate any moon cravings she had from now on.

He was worried about leaving her in the Motsi building, but he knew asking her to come home early was inviting an argument. He didn't think his entering the building would cause that much of a fuss, but he'd certainly had eyes on him while he'd been there. Even as he left, he could feel them watching. Cyrus Booth was plotting, that much was apparent, but it was nothing Dallas didn't warn them about.

Dusk was settling when he got the alert that she'd entered his gate, and he breathed out a sigh of relief. He'd worried that he'd been too rough on her earlier in her office. He turned toward his back door and waited for her. She exited, the suit jacket she wore to work missing. Her eyes were heated, feral. The light from her wolf flashed, and he smiled, crossing his arms over his chest.

"Hello, love."

She said nothing, simply pulling at the tie that held her dress together, gliding closer toward him. The fabric parted, exposing her beautiful skin. A white lace bra barely covered her breasts, and the panties he'd torn were gone, leaving her bare. His nostrils flared as the scent of her arousal reached him even over the smell of the sea traveling along the evening breeze. She pulled the bun from her hair, and her thick tresses fell to her shoulders and around her head in disarray. Shedding her dress altogether, she stopped in front of him.

His chest rumbled, his animal rising and filling his body. He gripped her chin and held her in place as he ravished her mouth. Keisha moaned, her hands grabbing his forearms. Her claws were out and digging into his skin. Devon's wolf swiped at him in impatience. Waiting until after their run to have her was out of the question.

Especially since she was reaching into his joggers. Once her hand closed around his dick, he was gone. He spun them around and lifted her to the railing. Giving in to his animal, he slid his claws along her thighs, growling in satisfaction at the welts lifting on her skin. No one but him would see the possessive marks, but their presence satiated a need deep inside him.

Fitting his dick at her center, he thrust inside. He swallowed a moan as her warmth surrounded his erection, squeezing down. He would go to his grave wanting this woman, worshipping this woman. She was crafted just for him, and as he pushed past her clenching walls to seat himself fully into his mate, Devon knew there would never be another for him.

"Goddamn," he couldn't help groaning.

She pulled back, her chest heaving as she gulped air. "What if someone—"

Devon cut off her words with another kiss. He didn't give a fuck at the moment. The beach was private enough. Besides, with the falling night, no one would pay attention to his house. He drove into her over and over, giving in to his animal's baser instincts. Wild, tenacious craving filled him, urging him to devour her. It took every ounce of his strength to keep his wolf from partially shifting.

Between the moon and the pleasure, he was damn near delirious. He pulled from her lips, his teeth scraping down the side of her neck. Her pussy squeezed him tight, stealing the last shreds of his control. Devon pushed in deeper, gripping her thighs as he basked in his mate.

"Bite me," she demanded, sucking on the skin of his shoulder.

He shook his head. "Not while you're drunk off the moon, mamas," he managed to say.

He would be devastated if she woke up regretting their actions. Keisha whimpered and nipped his skin. His wolf went wild, the temptation to bite her thrumming through his bloodstream. Frantic and uninhibited, Devon fucked his mate, losing himself in her.

"Ask me again tomorrow," he whispered harshly as his toes curled with his impending orgasm.

She grabbed the back of his head and brought him closer, biting down on his bottom lip, drawing blood. "One bite and I'm all yours," she taunted, arching her back to take him deeper.

Devon couldn't help the moan that escaped. Her aggression was the perfect match for him and his animal. His heart thumped hard against his chest, and his teeth dropped, his wolf howling in need. Her pussy clamped around his erection and his knees went weak.

Devon lifted her from the railing and sat on the first chair he saw, dropping her down on his dick. The moon shone bright behind her head, the power from her animal wrapped around him. Keisha rode him, her hips undulating on top of him. The hot clasp of her sheath pulled him under her spell, and he nearly gave in to her demand to seal their mating.

"Key," he pleaded.

She chuckled and licked across his bottom lip. "Fine, I'll wait until the morning."

He tried to be gentle, but his wolf refused to back down. He wanted to mark every inch of her as his. He bit her, careful not to break skin but growling in triumph at each imprint he left. Keisha did her own branding, her nails scoring his back. He hissed as she bit into his arm, her teeth leaving deep furrows.

"Possessive ass," he teased, driving deeper.

"You're mine," she stated emphatically.

Her claim was all it took to push him to the precipice. "Come for me," he demanded, unable to hold back any longer.

He reached down and pressed against her clit, hugging her tightly to him as his hips lifted, driving into her warm body. Keisha threw her head back, her mouth opening as she climaxed. The walls of her sex clenched against him, pulsing and pulling him down. He came hard, stars exploding behind his eyes.

"My wolf is ready to meet yours," she slurred, her head lying on his shoulder.

"Give me like...ten minutes, love," he husked out.

She giggled, and Devon could only smile. Love for her overwhelmed him, and all he could do was clutch her tightly.

19...

He gasped for air as he awakened in a sweat, his wolf aggressive and urgent against his skin, to the point where he could see fur pushing through his pores on his arms. He needed to run again, but half of him feared that if he started running, he would never stop. His property was big, but not that big. Fresh air, though, that would help.

Devon slid out of bed, pausing to make sure he didn't wake Keisha. She was sleeping soundly and had been since they'd showered after their run. His heart was still racing from his nightmare, and the only remedy for it was fresh air. He didn't bother throwing on clothes, happy to have the luxury of walking around in his shit any way he pleased. Grabbing his rolling tray from the bedside table, he headed outside.

The moment damp air hit his skin, his shoulders relaxed and his pulse slowed. He carefully climbed into the hammock hanging on his back porch and used the monotony of rolling a blunt to calm his mind. He'd been out for weeks, and yet the nightmares were still persistent. He could still hear the growls and screams of shifters behind bars, slowly going crazy as their animals were suppressed. Though he'd escaped that fate, it didn't stop his mind from replaying all he'd seen.

The sliding door opened just as he lit his blunt. Keisha padded over to him, a blanket wrapped around her nakedness.

"I can feel you," she said softly.

He waved his hand for her to come closer and set the tray down on the floor next to him. "What you mean?"

"I woke up out of a dead sleep because my wolf was urging me to come to you." She climbed on top of him in the hammock, sending it swinging.

He cuddled her close, dropping his lids to soak her in.

"You want me to call Patrice over here to check on you?"

He chuckled. "Don't do my mama." He lifted the lit blunt from the tray. "Is it okay with you if I smoke?"

"Of course."

He gripped her tight, her head resting against his chest as they both stared out into the night. The waves crashed against the shore, soothing the claustrophobia the nightmare brought to him. He rubbed her back, and it didn't take long for her animal to assuage the rough edges of his wolf. The animal still prowled his subconscious, but that need to destroy something had dimmed.

She kissed his skin. "Tell me."

He sighed before inhaling deep, holding the smoke in his lungs just a moment before releasing it. "Sometimes, I can feel the walls closing in around me. I thought being out six weeks would lessen that feeling, but the nightmares still catch me by surprise."

She hummed and rubbed her cheek against his chest. It was like she was marking her scent on his skin, and it caused his wolf to rumble his chest in approval.

"You need to call me when that happens."

"I wouldn't have to call you if your stubborn ass was where you're supposed to be."

She sighed. "I'm not even finna argue with you, Devon," she murmured, and he chuckled.

"I'm just saying, shawty."

They lay there in silence, and the longer they did, the calmer his animal was. He looked down when he felt Keisha's heavy breathing. Smiling, he woke her and helped her upstairs, back to his bed. He slid under the covers with her, pulling her into his chest. She traced her fingers along his skin where she left her teeth marks earlier.

"You marked my shit up," he said with a chuckle.

"You be in the hood too much for my peace of mind. I have to let them hoes know."

He snickered. "That explains why our scents are merged even though you haven't taken my bite. Possessive ass."

She sucked her teeth but didn't refute him.

"I ain't doing shit in the hood but getting them ready for my brother to take his place."

Her heart thumped in alarm. "I heard some rumors around the office."

"Oh, yeah?"

She sat up and stared down at him, bracing her hands on his chest. "They're trying to get you thrown back in."

"That's impossible, love. I'm not on parole. I did an extra two years so that I left that shithole free and clear. They ain't getting me on shit. Nothing will stop me from helping Declan claim what he wants."

She cupped his cheek. "You been watching out for him y'all whole life. It's admirable."

"We all we got," he said softly. "Or at least it used to be that way. Now we got mama and you."

She smiled, and he could see the sun radiate from that smile. He would never allow anyone to take him from her, no matter what that entailed. Devon would never tell his mate that and scare her, but it was the truth of the matter. He pulled her down and snuggled her.

"Sleep. You know you don't like missing work."

She sighed. "You right, I need to go. I don't have anything to wear here."

"I got clothes for you in the closet," he told her, turning so they were on their side.

"What? When?"

"The last time you came here, I felt unprepared, so I fixed it."

"If I wasn't so tired, I would look and see what you bought. You don't know my taste," she murmured, sliding her legs in between his to get comfortable.

He snorted. "Shiiid, the way I watch you, shawty? You buggin. Sleep," he ordered.

She rolled her eyes. "You so damn bossy, Devon."

"I'm too old to change, shawty."

She kissed his neck. "You live so far from the office."

"You want me to get you a driver?"

She studied him with her eyes narrowed.

"We both win. I have someone on you, and you get to look over work on your commute."

She didn't have to know that he'd already set it up for her to have a guard. Going into the Motsi building had given him an idea of what their life would be like. Her safety was a priority for him. It took her a while, and he held his breath, but she nodded.

"I hate driving, so it's fine with me. But a guard?"

"I already talked to Silas."

She growled. "Excuse you?"

"I had to make sure he could get into the building, shawty. What you want me to do, have him outside in the car all day?"

She sighed.

"He'll blend right into the security team Jules got set around y'all anyway. You won't even notice him except when you're coming and going home," he hurried to assure her.

"You're going to make him drive me here every night," she accused.

"I mean, hell yeah. But if you want to go home, he'll take you."

"Devon, you be doing too much."

"Compromise, love," he cajoled, sliding his leg against hers.

"Fine, then I want you to get security too. I'm not the one being shot at."

He kissed her pout. "I don't need security."

"Didn't you just say compromise?"

He chuckled, his fingers drifting down her body. She was warm and already wet for him.

"Just one, love. For me," she pleaded, and he knew he couldn't tell her no.

"I won't move around alone," he conceded. "Is that fine?"

She smiled, and his dick bucked against his thigh. Her pulse sped as her eyes lowered.

"I gotta be careful telling you yes for stuff because you always take advantage."

He laughed and slid inside her body. Closing his eyes, he let out a deep, satisfied breath. He would never tire of this woman. She arched into him, nuzzling into his neck.

"I love you, Keisha," he told her softly as he stroked her.

"Devon." Her breath hitched.

He chuckled. "You can deny it all you want, shawty, but I don't need the words from you. I feel it in the way you take care of me."

"I love you," she told him.

He kissed her deeply, taking that hard-fought confession from her.

She smiled and licked her lips, her canines extended. "Full moon's over. You can't say I'm moonstruck anymore."

He barely processed her words before she gripped his shoulder with her teeth, biting down. His wolf howled, and Devon moaned as her power filled him. She rocked her hips into his, and pleasure overtook him. He could feel her animal within him, his own rising to meet it. Keisha sucked on his skin, every pull scrambling his senses.

The need to taste her blood filled him and Devon gave in to the wolf, biting down on her shoulder. She didn't unlatch her teeth, instead biting down harder, making her mark deeper. Their animals roiled between them, bonding, blending their power until Devon and Keisha were melded together. The bond was tight, no hint of either of their insecurities, though he knew the morning could bring something different.

He prayed she wouldn't regret it.

He retracted his teeth, licking against the mark. Keisha finally released him, kissing his skin softly, humming in pleasure. He thrust into her body, his strokes slow and decadent now that he had her tied to him.

"I can feel you," she slurred, drunk off their combined power.

He closed his eyes, loving the feeling of her inside of him. He was privy to her thoughts and emotions and it pleased him. Her breath hitched and her pussy squeezed tighter as her orgasm swelled. He could feel his own as his dick expanded, his knot finally appearing with their mating. His wolf howled in victory and Devon's pleasure intensified as he came, his body locking to Keisha's. Extreme and profound bliss filled him, a sense of solace bringing tears to his eyes. Even knowing the knotting would happen, nothing prepared him for the peace of mind it gave him. Keisha moaned as her body tightened with another release, the hormones from the knotting flooding her system. She chanted his name, her back arched and her neck exposed to him in offering. Their bond unmasked them both and their every emotion was open to read.

He felt stripped bare. Keisha's arms went around his waist as she came down. It took nearly ten minutes before their animals relented, releasing his knot. Finally his erection softened, and he was able to carefully slide from her body. Keisha was asleep, her face tranquil. Chuckling, Devon stood and padded to his bathroom. He cleaned himself off, carrying out a washcloth to his mate. He wiped her body down, kissing her softly.

His animal was settled by the time he crawled back into bed with her, content that she was finally tied to them.

"Sleep, mamas," he murmured, pulling her into his arms.

"I love you," she whispered drowsily.

Devon buried his head between her neck and shoulder, holding in his tears. This woman was everything to him, and nothing would tear them apart.

20...

Keisha cursed under her breath as she swiped her card to enter the side of the building that housed Silas's offices. It housed all the offices for the felines. She was late, and it was all her mate's fault. Though…

She sighed. She had to take some of that blame. She could've showered alone, then maybe she would've made it to work on time. Living with Devon and having access to him was turning into an addiction for her. She couldn't keep her hands off him.

After weeks of waffling back and forth, Keisha was officially moved into Devon's house. Or rather, their house. She'd been very strict about leaving home on time to make work, but this morning, just the sight of him laid out in their bed distracted her. She was thankful Devon had insisted she have a driver because she was able to answer emails and schedule meetings the whole drive over.

Her phone dropped from her hand as she ran into someone.

"Crap." She stooped to grab it, sucking in a breath when she looked up at who she'd run into. "Councilman Booth. My apologies, I wasn't watching where I was going."

His flinty gaze raked her figure before coming back to her face. "Keisha Calhoun, right?"

She nodded and stepped to move around him. "If you'll excuse me, I'm running late."

He continued to stare, and for a moment, she didn't think he would allow her to pass. He was a tall man, built like most wolves; there wasn't a lot of muscle on his body, but she knew that could be deceiving. His salt and pepper hair was cut low, and the three-piece suit he wore looked tailored to his body. His attire and carefully groomed appearance showcased his money. At first glance, he could be mistaken for nonchalant, soft even. One look into his dark eyes and that whole façade was thrown away.

"Newly mated, huh? Interesting," he finally said.

Keisha stopped trying to pass him and froze, frowning at him.

"Your father was Leland Calhoun. He was a big name on the West side. Shame what happened to him." The smile he gave her didn't reach his eyes. "It's the same old story when a street thug tries to get involved in things above their station."

Her wolf bucked and she debated whether to say anything. She'd never been one to bite her tongue, but talking reckless to a councilman was not a good idea. Before she could make up her mind, Councilman Knight rounded the corner with the two security guards that always flanked him. Cyrus Booth was powerful, but Dallas Knight was a whole other animal. From the way he moved through a space to the cunning in his eyes, everything about him screamed predator. Even the guards with Councilman Booth stood taller in his presence.

"Good morning, Keisha." Dallas looked at Cyrus and his eyes hardened. "We got a problem?"

Keisha shook her head quickly, praying to prevent a confrontation between the two men. Everyone in the building knew they didn't get along.

"No, everything is fine with me."

Dallas's gaze never left Cyrus. "The fuck you doing on this side of the building?"

"Damn, I can't even walk around? Cold world," Cyrus said before shooting her a parting look.

She shuddered at the malice she saw there. Dallas stepped closer to her. "Where's your security?"

"He's parking," she answered, wincing.

While she was happy to have a driver, she was still getting used to moving around with security. There were times, like now, when she completely forgot that he was supposed to shadow her everywhere.

"I was running late," she tried to explain.

Dallas held up his hand to stop her words. "Don't do that again, understand?"

She nodded, taken aback by the worry in his gaze. "Yes, sir."

"Devon will burn all this shit down behind you, so you gotta move better from now on, hear?"

"Of course," she said, chastised.

"Walk her to Silas's office," Dallas ordered his second security guard.

"Oh, that's…" She closed her mouth at the look he cut her. "Thank you," she murmured and followed behind the massive panther shifter.

Silas was waiting for her at the door when she got to the office. "What happened?"

She sighed in relief to be in safety. "Ran into Councilman Booth."

"He say anything?"

"No, just commented on my mating," she lied.

Silas cursed and pulled out his phone.

"Please do not text Devon." She could well imagine what he would do if he came down. "It was just words, Silas."

Silas grunted and inclined his head for her to follow him. "You need to hire an assistant."

She frowned. "What? Why?"

"Keisha, you're swamped, mama, and now mated. Your work/home balance needs to get better. Congratulations, by the way," he said, stopping at her office.

"Thank you. And I know you aren't talking."

He chuckled. "Hey, I've slowed down since Mila and Riyah have come into my life."

"Which means I have too," she argued.

"No, because you're still managing me and this office. Pick one and hire someone for the other."

She frowned. "I don't want an office manager messing up my system."

"Then train them, duh."

Rock snickered as he came up to them. He leaned down and whispered something in Silas's ear. It must've had to do with her because Silas studied her, nodding to whatever he'd said. They both looked at her when he was done.

"What?"

"Congratulations," Rock said, ignoring her question.

Her eyes narrowed. "Fine. Keep your secrets."

She left them standing there and entered her office. She'd told Silas not to call Devon, but she debated it herself. She wanted his opinion on what Councilman Booth had said. She had a feeling that the whole thing was layered in subtext. Did he know something about why her father had died? Had he been involved? She chewed her lip because if she told Devon that Cyrus had confronted her, he would likely do as Councilman Knight said and come in here, guns blazing. Still, she couldn't expect him to share with her if she wasn't willing to do the same. Making the decision, she pulled out her phone.

"Hey, mamas," he greeted.

"I'm safe in the office," she reported, and he grunted. "So, I just ran into Councilman Booth."

"Did he say something?"

"He did, and it got my mind thinking."

Devon cursed. "About what?"

She could feel his agitation through their bond. "He said that what happened to my father was what happened when street thugs got involved above their station."

His growl rattled the phone. "You think it was a warning?"

"I also think he was telling on himself. Otherwise, why bring up daddy?"

"That motherfucker. Your guard was near?"

"I'm safe," she said instead, not wanting to lie to him.

He sighed. "Be careful moving around that building, hardheaded. Declan's calling me, so I gotta go. I love you."

"I love you too." She hung up.

She'd barely had time to start any work when Silas walked back into her office almost forty-five minutes later. He closed her door behind him.

"What's wrong?"

"You have to go home early." Silas looked serious.

"What? Silas, you have meetings all day." Confusion had her brows bunched.

"Keisha, some shit about to go down and you need to be out of the building," he explained.

Her phone vibrated across her desk, but she sent it to voicemail. "We should be safe here. I have my guard, and Rocco is here."

Silas sighed. "Keisha."

Rocco interrupted whatever he was going to say by opening her office door. "It's too late."

Silas cursed, and butterflies fluttered in her stomach. What the hell was going on? This time when her phone rang, she answered because she knew Devon would keep calling until she did.

"I can't talk right now, babe."

"Key, you in Silas's office?" The urgency in his voice paused her.

"Yes. What's wrong?" she asked, exasperated.

"Stay there," he ordered.

Lord have mercy. "What is going on, Dev?"

"Declan is making his play today. I'm outside the Motsi building waiting on him."

"Why didn't you say anything this morning?" Shock had her hands shaking.

"He just called me while I was on the phone with you, love."

"Ok. Please be careful," she told him. She didn't want to distract him by arguing.

"Always, love," he said and hung up.

Silas and Rock left her office, and for a moment, she didn't know what to do. Not that she didn't think Declan could win, but the danger that she knew it posed for Declan and Devon both...

Julissa rushed into her office. "Girl! The Ursa side is jumping. Did you know Declan was going to make his move today?"

She stood on shaky legs and shook her head. Not knowing what was going on would send her spiraling. She wasn't supposed to leave the office, but... "Let's go, we can sneak and look." She picked up her tablet.

She and Julissa rushed from her office, but Rock stopped them as they headed for the door, grabbing his wife around the waist. "Aht-aht. Keep your nosy ass right here so I can keep my eyes on you both."

Julissa protested. "It won't be a fight today, and we were just going to..."

"What I say, Liss?" he said gruffly.

"You not mad they left you back to watch the women?" Julissa taunted, and her mate's eyes flashed with his bear.

Keisha bit her lip to keep from laughing because her friend had no sense of self-preservation; she knew that Rock would make Julissa pay for that comment. He seemed to sense her amusement and turned to Keisha, and she held up her hands. Keisha recognized that look in Rock's eyes. She'd seen it in Devon's gaze enough to know the bear wouldn't budge on his stance.

She gave Julissa a look, and the two of them headed for the small conference room within Silas's suite. Rock narrowed his eyes but was otherwise silent. They rushed in the room and shut the door. She whipped out her phone and dialed the one number she could count on to help.

"Hey, Deena," she greeted as Julian's mate answered her phone.

She'd met Julian's mate before when she went to gatherings at Silas's house. The two of them had quickly bonded since Julian worked so closely with Silas. A friendship between them had been easy.

"He locked you in a room?"

"Damn near," she whined.

"You gotta train him better, Key, or Devon will have you locked up at the house next to me and Celine," Deena lamented.

She snorted in amusement. "I want to see what's going on. Do you think Julian will allow us to see the surveillance?"

Deena sucked her teeth. "They're so aggy, I don't know if he'll allow it. Mason has us at the ranch, with Lance and Noah standing by the door looking ferocious as though we're going to sneak away."

"Can you ask nicely?" Keisha cajoled.

Deena laughed. "Let me see what I can do."

She hung up, and Keisha shrugged at Julissa. About five minutes later, Rock came in. She and Julissa both looked up in guilt and he shook his head. He took her tablet, going through a couple different screens before footage from the CCTV in the Motsi building came up.

"That's too small," Julissa said impatiently over her shoulder.

"You right." Keisha pressed a button, and a projector screen descended from the ceiling. Rock shared her screen and it came up big. Her heart thumped when her mate and his brother came through the front door.

Both brothers were dressed in all black. The last time Keisha had seen Devon in a suit was on their date night. God almighty, that man was fine as hell. He wore power like a second skin; it translated even through the surveillance video. She shuddered to think how that power would feel in person.

The Edwards brothers didn't come in alone. She recognized some of the wolves who used to work for her father behind them. She knew that Devon would've rather had Jules and Silas next to him, but his friends had to remain neutral. It didn't stop them from being in the building, though. She saw both men coming from the feline hallway as they stopped at the end to watch.

"We need audio," she murmured.

She watched the screen with bated breath, praying harder than she'd ever prayed in her life. She probed her mating bond, relaxing as she realized there was no fear in her mate. She put her faith in him. The only thing she could do was await the outcome.

21...

The crowd gathering riled Devon's wolf. Little stings of electricity danced across his skin as the animal paced his body, ready for action. He stood next to his brother, his arms crossed over his chest. Three of the soldiers that had always been on Devon's team stood at their back, along with his brother's security. Drew had offered to come, but Devon turned him down. Declan was ready to roll, so he'd called up people he knew could reach him in time.

"I'm here to challenge Cyrus Booth for the wolf council seat!" Declan called out.

Devon's eyes swept the elegant lobby. He'd barely paid attention last time because his mate was his sole focus. Now, though, he glanced at the high ceilings and white marble floors. The light fixtures were art all on their own. The white metal mesh looked like ribbons of fabric swirling along the ceilings. Coupled with the glass entrance, it felt like being inside a museum. The delicate décor juxtaposed against the aggressive energy from the shifters inside was jarring. There were three separate corridors with their own guard stations off from the lobby. The entrances were filled with curious shifters.

The two security guards that had been at the door had now multiplied to ten, standing in front of Devon and Declan and the hittas behind them.

"We can't let you in any further." One of the guards stepped forward.

Devon had to give him props because no fear emanated from him. Clearly, the Motsi didn't hire pussies like he thought. A hush went through the crowd as a large bear shifter pushed through the people clogging the Ursa entrance. Devon knew who he was; he'd studied the councilmembers when his brother had announced his intention. Councilman Micah Crespo walked up to them, analyzing his brother.

"There are procedures that have to be followed for challenges." His deep voice filled the silence of the lobby.

"Ain't I here in this lobby declaring my intention instead of showing up to his house and dragging him out?" Declan told him.

The bear's lips quirked up before he completely hid his smile. "Then follow me, gentlemen."

He led them from the lobby into a clear conference room, where another bear Devon assumed was Crespo's second was already waiting. Everyone could see into that motherfucker, so that reassured Devon they wouldn't be on no bullshit. The door opened and Dallas and Julian Senior walked in, moving to stand next to the bear and his second.

"Where is he?" Declan asked.

"Probably hiding. Ol' bitch ass," Dallas commented, and Senior laughed.

The bear once again covered his amusement. "I've sent a runner to him."

"How we finna do this then?" Devon asked, already tired of the theater.

"We'll formally announce the challenge. Cyrus will set his terms, and if you agree to them, then we will proceed."

"Would've been faster to come in here and air the whole bitch out," Devon grumbled, and the bear shot him a hard look.

Crespo cut a look to Dallas. "That would've worked once upon a time. Nowadays, since the last two challengers came in slaughtering whole courts, the rules have changed."

Dallas smirked, not at all repentant for how he took his seat.

They waited in tense silence. It didn't take long for Cyrus to bust into the door.

"'Bout time. Almost thought you would take the cowardly way out," Senior said, leaning back in the chair where he sat.

"Call me one more fucking coward," Booth hissed.

Senior smiled, his canines low. "What, pray tell, would you do about it, bitch?"

Crespo held up his hand. "Let's get this over with please. Cyrus, this gentleman…"

"Declan Edwards," his brother answered.

"Declan Edwards has extended a challenge for your position," Crespo told him.

"On what grounds?" the wolf next to Cyrus spoke up.

"Just because, pussy ass ho," Devon snapped, to which Senior and Dallas snickered.

Crespo sighed. "Cyrus, you have three weeks to answer the challenge in the affirmative or give up your position."

Cyrus growled. "I accept."

Crespo nodded his head. "Fine, then. Three weeks from today, we'll meet back here for the challenge. On challenge day, regardless of who wins, any other challenger is allowed to step forward until the last wolf is standing. Is that understood by both?"

His brother and Cyrus both nodded.

"It should be noted how it would look if anything happens to Declan prior to the challenge," Dallas said casually.

Cyrus's eyes lit with his wolf. "What the fuck are you implying, Dallas Knight?"

Dallas shrugged. "Take it how you want to."

"Alright, challenge accepted, meeting the fuck over. Cyrus, you leave first," Crespo ordered.

"Be seeing you," Declan taunted as the other wolves filed out.

Once they'd left the building, Devon stopped his brother before he got into his car. "I thought you were waiting?"

"I was shooting the shit with Deena and Julian let slip that you thought Cyrus was behind your setup," Declan answered. He rubbed a hand over his head. "If that's the case, then he gotta go sooner than I planned."

Devon nodded, acknowledging the anger on his brother's face. "There's no proof."

"I don't give a fuck," Declan snapped. "I'm not sitting back and waiting on him to do some shit to you again."

"You sound like Key," he said, smiling at his brother.

"I just got you back, Dev. I'm not trying to lose you," Declan said, pulling him into a hug. "Stay safe, big brother."

"Always. The target's on you now," he reminded him.

Declan nodded. "I'm aware. I'll get up with you later."

Devon watched his brother leave. He pulled out his phone and texted Silas, telling him it was safe to send his mate out. He didn't want her in the building today. Dallas had called him earlier and told him what happened in the hallway, warning him that it would be a good idea to increase protection over his mate. When Dallas had taken his seat, it had been violent, but Cyrus had put that to shame, and not in an honorable way. He'd slaughtered nearly the whole Cartwright family until Micah Crespo had intervened.

Shifters were violent, there was no denying that, but the Motsi had been able to contain most of the brutality with its creation. Power brought out the most greedy of any society, and the Motsi were no different. The amount of power the council held was temptation to any shifter. Keisha walking out of the building broke into his thoughts.

She was so fucking sexy. Fate did their big one with his mate. She was crafted just for him, molded to perfection and wrapped in the most beautiful melanin. The teal suit pants and matching vest hugged her curves and made his mouth water. She'd been surprised to see the designer outfits he'd filled his closet with for her. He kept mum about getting the shopper at Knights' to help. She didn't need to know that. She praised his good taste and happily wore the clothes. That was all he could ask for.

"I still have to work," she warned him as she walked up to him.

"You can do it from home," he assured her, pulling her into his arms. He probed their bond, sensing her anxiety, and used his wolf to calm her. She cupped his cheek, her worried gaze tracing his face.

"I'm good, love. This is it; the gauntlet has been laid down. I understand what that means, and I will keep myself safe."

She nodded and kissed him softly. "Okay. I didn't have time to eat this morning, so stop on the way home."

"Yes, ma'am," he chuckled. He kissed her again, unable to resist deepening it.

Devon helped her into his truck and drove them to Mrs. B's. It was his favorite restaurant, and ever since he'd been out, he'd made more than one visit. He was happy his brother had invested in the restaurant on his behalf. He didn't want to see a hood staple driven away by gentrification. Opening Keisha's door, he helped her out, licking his lips.

"You got that shit on, mamas," he said, skimming her hips.

She smiled. "You did good."

The place was crowded despite it being between breakfast and lunch. He was greeted warmly as they walked in. The interior hadn't changed much, though he could see that they'd updated the place. It looked like most mom-and-pop diners. A leather bench spanned the brick wall from the door to the counter, small tables in front of it with a single chair in front of each table for small groups. Five four-seater tables were on the opposite side of that, leaving an aisle from the front door to the counter to order. There were framed pictures of local celebrities on the wall, and the scent of fried food wafted to them.

"I haven't been here in years," Keisha murmured with a smile, her eyes swiping through the menu on the wall over the registers.

"Devon. What it do, playboy?"

He turned and spotted Drew leaving his table and walking toward them. They dapped in greeting.

"Key, this is my friend, Drew. Drew, my baby, Keisha."

Keisha held out her hand. "I remember you. You used to work for daddy as well."

Drew smiled, shaking her hand. "Yep. I'm sorry for your loss."

Keisha nodded, stepping away to allow them to talk in private. Devon and Drew also moved out of the line and to the side to keep the conversation to themselves.

"I got a meeting for you tomorrow," Drew told him.

"With who?"

"I finally got in contact with Talon's crew and requested a meeting."

"Word?" Devon nodded.

Talon's crew ran guns through town and were a big gang on the West side. Devon had no intentions of promising them anything, but he did want to see if they were on Cyrus's side or not. Crespo said that any challengers to the seat could step forward, and he wanted to make sure that no one from Talon's gang would be in that number. He wasn't worried about shit when it came to his brother, but he would cover Declan's ass where he could. Plus, they were a good contact to have. Even Cartwright with his uptightness had understood that having the streets behind him increased the length of his reign. Though in the end, Cyrus had given no warning when he struck, rendering any help Leland could've provided useless.

Devon would ensure nothing like that happened with his brother.

"Bet. Text me the address and time."

Drew nodded toward Keisha. "Didn't see that coming."

"That's my baby," he said.

"That's what's up. Be easy."

"What was that about?" Keisha asked as he joined her in line.

He wrapped his arms around her and nuzzled into her neck. "Nothing for you to worry about."

"Devon..."

"I gotta wrap this shit up, mamas. That's it. I swear. I'll tell you about it when we get home and away from prying eyes."

She nodded. "I'm holding you to your word."

He knew she meant it. His next meeting would be one of the last. He'd already gone to his safe deposit box and got the black book that held all of Leland's contacts and information. He would turn it over to Drew, make the necessary introductions, and that would be the end of his involvement.

22...

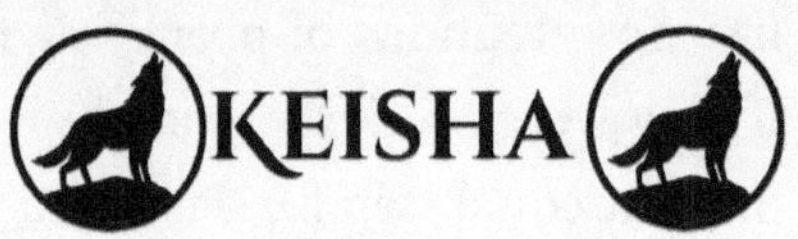

Keisha took a deep breath and slid her dress up her legs. Her stomach was cramping, and she was not in the mood to schmooze the attendants of tonight's fundraiser. She'd barely been able to keep her face straight while she'd sat in the stylist's chair. She normally would joke and catch up on gossip, but her mood had been sour all day.

Not a lot of work needed to be done at the event. She, Mila, and the eldest Mrs. Knight had done everything they needed to early in the day, leaving the rest to the party planner. It still hadn't stopped Keisha's phone from ringing while she was getting hair and makeup done. It was the same every year, last minute RSVPs and plus-one changes. Julian threatened to throttle her if she sent him one more background request. It was required due to the caliber of people attending.

She growled as she tried to zip her dress. The back had a high neck, the zipper spanning from just above her hip all the way to the top of the dress. Seeming to sense her aggravation, Devon appeared at their bedroom door. The designer tux fit his body perfectly, the navy-blue color matching her gown. She sucked in a surprised breath. His hair was freshly cut, the line up sharp and framing his face. He looked like a god.

"Need help?"

She nodded, unable to speak, and turned her body, giving him her back. The satin gown was fitted and long-sleeved, with a scoop neck cut out in the front. It was sedate and elegant, appropriate for the event and her position. She never wanted to stand out at these types of events.

Devon leaned down and kissed her nape exposed from her updo. She shivered and her animal roiled within her body. The soft touch of his fingers on her skin had her closing her eyes tight. He zipped her in and pulled her back into his arms. As he inhaled her hair, his wolf rubbed against hers in a soothing manner.

"What's wrong?"

"I'm good," she said.

Devon spun her around and studied her face. Her phone rang and she cursed under her breath, even while she was relieved for the distraction. She knew from experience that Devon would've called her out on her lie.

"I need to take this," she whispered, avoiding his gaze.

He grunted but left her to it.

By the time she finished fussing with the caterer, she was fed up with it all. Not that she could reschedule a yearly event around her period, but God, she wished she could stay home. She came down the stairs to find Devon at the kitchen island sipping his favorite bourbon. She knew it was irrational, but seeing him relaxed when she felt so out of control and harried pissed her off.

"We need to go," she snapped.

Devon raised an eyebrow, not moving as they stared at each other in tense silence. The power of his wolf rose, his dominance blanketing her. Hers whined in response.

"I'm sorry. I don't want to take my mood out on you," she said through tight lips.

He finally broke his gaze, standing and carrying his glass to his sink. "You been doing that shit all day." He rinsed the glass and set it in the dishwasher, and again, something about his nonchalance set her off.

"My phone been ringing all damn day, Devon. Excuse me if it's made me irritable."

He stalked closer to her, and she swallowed hard but stood her ground, even as her animal wanted her to expose her throat to him.

"You need to check your attitude before I actually get pissed off, love." He gripped her chin softly. "I don't disrespect you. Return the favor."

She nodded, his chastising her making her emotional. He turned, saying nothing else, and headed toward the front door. The guard he'd assigned her was standing next to his Range Rover in the driver's spot. Devon waved him off as he came to help them in, opening the back door for Keisha.

"Get in the car," he ordered.

She stomped over, mumbling her thanks as he held the door open before sliding in next to her. He reached over and buckled her in, kissing her shoulder, sending her hormones more out of control.

"I'ma let all that earlier shit slide because I can feel you in pain despite you keeping that shit from me."

He closed the door, and she kept her face to the window and fought to get her emotions under control. By the time they'd pulled up to the hotel where the fundraiser was being held, she'd worked herself up even more, the deep breaths not working to calm her.

Devon growled next to her. "Don't start all that crying shit neither," he fussed. "Fix your face so we can get this over with and I can feed your stubborn ass. With the way my animal is feeling, if one person tries to step in like I'm doing something to you, I'ma kick all this shit over."

God, he was so ridiculous. His words should've felt harsh, but the authority in his tone shook her out of her mood. She couldn't help the chuckle of amusement that left her mouth. That's what she got for thinking this man was going to baby her.

"Fine, Devon," she muttered.

He got out first, looking around before he helped her out.

She stepped into his heated body, unable to resist the comfort of his presence. "An hour, two tops."

He nodded, running his warm hands down her back. Her body shuddered and her wolf spun within her, reveling in his touch. She looked toward the looming hotel, sighing at the crowd of people waiting to go in. The Crown Hotel and Spa was a popular venue for events and would comfortably hold the six hundred guests that were attending tonight's fundraiser.

"I want to go home."

He leaned down. "Let's go, then. I can take care of you when we get there."

She closed her eyes as he kissed her softly. "That sounds so good. But I need to show my face." Especially after all the work she'd put in. "Silas won't mind if I leave early, though."

He turned their bodies toward the venue. "Come on. I need to scope this shit out anyways."

Butterflies attacked her stomach at his statement. She'd gotten a few last-minute RSVPs from the wolf council and now, she definitely didn't want to go in. She nodded and reluctantly separated their bodies, grabbing his hand. They walked through security after Keisha showed her invitation.

"Damn, they not checking for guns or nothing, huh?" he whispered in her ear.

"This ain't that type of event," she said dryly.

"All the better for me," he said, and she glanced at him, already knowing he was toting.

"Please do not pull your gun out on anyone. Julian will be very upset."

He chuckled. "Jules knows how I move."

"Lord have mercy," she said under her breath as they entered the banquet hall. The drop ceilings were high, crystal chandeliers hanging from each square. Tables filled the room, the white table linens matching the chairs. The centerpieces were beautifully crafted, the lilies standing out. An area for dancing was in the center of the room, the tables surrounding it. The stage was small, which was fine since only Silas would be speaking tonight.

She spotted Silas right away and headed in that direction. "I'll need to work."

"I understand, Key," he told her. "I know how to act, love."

She snorted. "Since when?"

She was relieved the earlier tension was broken and they were back on even ground. Her eyes traced the ballroom, double-checking details that she'd gone through when she'd been here earlier in the day. Everything was as it was supposed to be. The caterer had figured out the champagne problem, and waiters were circulating as they should. Her shoulders slightly relaxed, knowing the hard part was done.

Silas and Mila were standing near the entrance and greeted them both as they walked up. Silas wore a dark red tuxedo and his wife was in a strapless ball gown of the same color, the heavy brocade fabric flaring into a beautiful full skirt. She looked like a queen. Silas grabbed Devon into a hug, their closeness evident to anyone looking. Devon had explained to her how they grew up together, and she loved that her mate still had his friends even after everything he'd been through. She pulled her mini tablet from her bag and pulled up the guest list for tonight, glancing over it as she got ready to play her part.

"You look beautiful, Keisha," Mila greeted her, rubbing their cheeks together.

"Thank you, so do you." A genuine smile lifted her lips.

Mila locked arms with her. "You'll have to guide me through this. It's my first time being hostess."

Adina had finally given the reins over to her daughter-in-law, and as far as Keisha could tell, Mila was a natural. The woman was friendly and charming, and that would go a long way to loosening pockets.

"Well, first things first, we need to be at the door, greeting the guests as they come in."

Mila nodded. "Silas, time to work, my love."

He dapped Devon again and came to his wife's side. Devon grabbed her from Mila and planted a kiss on her forehead.

"Let me know if you need anything, hear?"

She nodded.

"Devon, perfect timing." Councilman Knight walked up to the group and greeted his son and daughter-in-law. "I got some people I want you to meet."

Devon kissed her temple and walked off with Councilman Knight, leaving Keisha to her duties. She took a deep breath and got into work mode, taking her place behind the Knights. She was only there for support. Silas rarely forgot people, so her job was easy. She whispered to Mila when there were specific donors with whom she needed to pour on the charm.

She smiled as Declan came through the receiving line. They'd met more than once in Silas's office, so she was already aware of him prior to mating with his brother. He was always congenial when he visited and never one of those kinds of people who overlooked staff members. He knew who her father was and had always treated her as most people on the West side did, with a little aloofness but respect. Even after Leland's death, his reputation had kept her and her mother safe.

He greeted the couple, his gaze going straight to Keisha, then stepped past Silas. "Let me greet my new sister properly."

He lightly touched their foreheads together before pulling her into his arms. His greeting was warmer, signaling the change in their relationship now that she'd mated with his brother.

"Hi, Declan," she greeted him.

"Where's your mate?"

She looked around but didn't spot him among the crowd. "He took off with Councilman Knight."

"I'll catch up with him," he told her, kissing her forehead and walking off.

Despite the fact that her body was aching, time passed fast. They'd finished the receiving line and she floated around with Silas, making appointments and notes as he dictated. He used the fundraiser well, gauging concerns from the shifters he represented. The event was full of rich shifters, but Silas would also hold a few different town halls to make sure that he reached those who wouldn't be shelling out ten thousand dollars a plate to be heard.

She loved working for him for that reason. He was great at his job, and she enjoyed helping fellow shifters.

Another hour into the event, her stomach started cramping, and the energy she'd been able to find was slowly dwindling. Though they were only mated for days, Devon read her well, appearing out of thin air at her side.

23...

Devon grabbed Keisha's elbow. "You need a break."

It wasn't a question. His wolf was pacing his body as the pain she tried to hide from him leaked into their bond. Keisha was able to hide her discomfort well, but he was fed up with allowing it.

He'd been watching her from across the room as Mr. D circled him through the crowd, introducing him to council staff. It was part of the dance he would soon be doing on behalf of his brother. He'd made it his business to learn more about the inner workings of the Motsi since he'd been out. He knew who the different members of the council were, and with Mr. D's help, he was able to fill in the blanks.

She didn't argue with his order, simply excusing herself and following him as he pushed through the crowd. Keisha sighed in relief as Devon guided her to an upholstered bench in a dimly lit alcove. He handed her a bottle of water, nodding for her to sit. She did as ordered, laying the cold plastic of the bottle against the back of her neck. His sharp gaze raked over her, but he said nothing.

"Thank you," she whispered.

He grunted and pulled out his phone, sending a message to his brother that he was getting ready to head out. He didn't know how much longer Silas needed Keisha, but he was anxious to get her home. She was silent as she sipped at her water, and he let her have a moment. The murmur of the crowd still filled the air, but here, in this little corner, the noise was decidedly less. Declan rounded the pillars separating them from the rest of the room a few minutes later, his eyes finding Keisha.

"What's wrong?" he asked.

She shook her head. "Just taking a break."

He eyed her a moment before turning his attention to his brother. "I need a smoke."

Declan sat down next to Keisha, pulling a blunt from his tuxedo jacket. Devon growled, and his brother sucked his teeth.

"You been mated ten minutes, please take your tender dick ass on."

Devon flipped him off. "Put some space between you and my mate."

Declan ignored him, and Keisha chuckled at their bickering. Despite the fact that he was aggravated, Devon missed these little moments with his brother.

"There's no smoking in here," Keisha said when Declan pulled out his lighter.

"You can't make an exception for me, sis? My wolf about to lose his shit."

She laughed, stretching out her legs. "This ain't my personal house to be making no exception for you."

Declan lit up anyway, and Keisha rolled her eyes. Devon shook his head at his brother because in the years they'd been separated, Declan had changed from a sensitive, shy teenager to this arrogant male before him. He liked it.

The hair on the back of his neck raised, his wolf warning him of impending danger. Declan seemed to sense it at the same time. They both straightened their postures and growled as Keisha looked around for what had upset them.

Councilman Booth and his second came around the corner. Cyrus raked the brothers with a derisive look before his gaze went to Keisha.

"No wonder you were able to get in. I can't imagine the prison paid you enough to afford the ticket price for this fundraiser."

Devon chuckled. "Them bars didn't stop my bag. Despite being set up by a coward, my name still gets loyalty. I'm sure you realized that when you were trying to move shit through my streets."

Devon smiled as Cyrus's eyes flashed with his wolf. Despite his age, the councilman was still powerful, but that shit didn't move him.

"The fuck you come over here for?" Declan asked, pulling on his blunt, his whole demeanor unbothered. "We ain't got shit to say to each other for another two weeks."

"Anything could happen between now and then," Cyrus taunted.

Devon stepped closer to Cyrus and growled. "You fucking right about that. Anyone can be touched. Remember that when you sleep tonight in that big ass mansion off Cliff House Lane."

Cyrus stiffened but held up his hand to stop his second from reacting. "You two stay safe out here," he finally said, walking off.

"I can't wait to kill him," Declan said, blowing smoke into the air.

Devon grunted in agreement. He wished he could feel his claws dig into Cyrus's neck. Especially if he was the one who set up Leland. His gaze strayed to his mate as she swiped a shaking hand over her hair. He probed their bond, feeling her anxiety. It was time for them to go.

"Come on, mamas," he ordered her gently. "Stay out of trouble," he told his brother.

Declan chuckled. "I'm out too."

The three of them made their way to the exit. Declan's car came through the valet first, and he dapped his brother.

"You need to come by the house for dinner."

Declan smiled. "We doing family dinners now?"

"You'll be where the fuck I tell you to be," Devon teased his little brother.

"Yeah, a'ight. Be easy, sister." Declan nuzzled the top of Keisha's head and swaggered to his car.

Devon pulled Keisha into his arms, her body tense with pain. "Hurting?" he murmured against her skin.

She nodded, her face a polite mask.

"Did you take anything before you left the house?" She shook her head, and he sighed. "Hardheaded ass." He couldn't resist leaning down and kissing the pout from her mouth.

He pulled out his phone and ordered them food to be delivered to the house by the time they reached it. Knowing her, she'd worked through the whole event without taking time for herself. He helped her into his truck and drove them home.

She was half-asleep by the time he pulled into the garage. He carried her to their bedroom, setting her down on the edge of the bed. He shed his tuxedo jacket as he headed to the shower. Starting the hot water, he pulled aspirin out of the medicine cabinet. There was a small beverage fridge next to their bed. He handed her a bottle of water and shook the aspirin into her hands.

"Dev," she said softly.

Her eyes followed him across the room. Grabbing one of his t-shirts and her underwear, he inclined his head for her to follow him into the bathroom.

"Did you eat anything tonight?"

She shook her head, wincing as she downed the pills. Just as he suspected. He turned her so he could unzip her dress. Resting a hand on her bare shoulder, he inhaled her hair, the smell of some type of blossom making him hard. He shook himself, remembering that she was hurting. He unzipped her dress with shaking hands, longing and hunger for her mixed in with his need to care for her.

Keisha held her dress to her chest and turned. He kissed the tip of her upturned nose. She took his breath away, and it had nothing to do with her beauty. The vulnerable softness in her eyes made him want to wrap her in affection and baby her.

"Take your time," he whispered, kissing her full lips softly.

Her eyes searched his face before she stepped back. He left her to shower alone, knowing he wasn't in a place to see her naked and act right. He hopped in one of the guest bathrooms, taking a quick shower. The food arrived as he finished, and he hurried downstairs to grab it. He'd ordered her wings, a small salad, and a giant slice of lemon cake, things he'd knew she'd like from their many conversations.

Devon set up a tray of food for her on the small coffee table between the armchairs in the sitting area of their room.

He looked up as the bathroom door opened. Steam preceded her, the light from the bathroom painting her silhouette beneath his shirt. His pulse stuttered and his wolf roamed his body, its power raising the hair on his arms. Keisha padded over to him, her eyes on his dick. He knew it was tenting the towel he had slung around his waist but wasn't shit he could do about that.

Her wolf rumbled her chest, and he couldn't help the cocky smile that tilted his lips. The heat in her eyes matched his own and that satisfied him deeply.

"Come eat, love," he beckoned.

Once he had her situated in the chair, he went to change. He slid on a pair of underwear, hoping the barrier would signal to his wolf that this was about taking care of their mate. He sat next to her, putting on an old movie as they ate. A part of him sensed her need for quiet, so he said nothing, simply cleaning up after them when she was done eating.

By the time he came from dumping their trash, he found her in the middle of the bed, her eyes heavy with sleep. Her pain had lessened, the heavy feeling of it gone from their bond. He settled against the headboard and pulled her between his legs. He kissed the top of her head and slid his hand against her stomach. No words were exchanged, but Keisha wiggled until she found a comfortable spot.

"Thank you, love," she said quietly, her arms wrapping around him.

Her breathing deepened a few moments later, and he smiled as she finally went to sleep. It was the simple pleasures that had him looking forward to years with his mate.

24...

The meeting with Drew should've been easy enough. The two friends met at the café so that Devon could answer any final questions Drew had about taking over. He'd already introduced him to the plug and shared the contacts Drew would need to keep the business going. He'd even extracted a promise from his friend to support Declan in the upcoming challenge.

He had no doubt his brother could defeat Cyrus, but there was always what came after. Changes in power always shook up a city, and Eastfield would be no different. Devon wanted his brother covered in case someone tried to jump stupid once the challenge was won. He'd been expecting the morning to be easy and quick. Nothing prepared him to be the target of an attack.

That was his bad.

Somewhere between the first and the fourth shot fired at him, Devon realized that even though he was in the process of changing his life, he would still need to be on his p's and q's. He shifted quickly, tearing through his clothes as his body expanded and cursing the fact that he would be leaving behind his wallet. His wolf had no such regrets or thoughts for that matter. The animal was single-minded, and survival was its only thought as he leaped for his attacker.

The man got off one more shot before Devon was on him, claws penetrating his belly through the layers of clothes he wore. Devon had enough control for the wolf to make sure he aimed his claws low enough to reach beneath his attacker's bulletproof vest. His claws pierced him and raked through meat and organs. The man screamed and fell to the ground, the other with him scrambling to get away as Devon took down another one. He used that man's body to shield him, taking the impact from the bullets as another male shot at him. Devon tossed the corpse aside the moment he heard the click of the empty clip, jumping on the shooter.

He didn't even have time to figure out why he was being attacked.

The fact that they weren't even across the tracks was really what had Devon confused because who the fuck would come after him in broad daylight near downtown Eastfield? It didn't matter the answer as he killed another one of the men after him. His wolf growled in satisfaction as he ripped this one's throat out.

"Let's go, D!" Drew yelled from down the street where they'd parked.

The sounds of oncoming sirens filtered through his anger and the wolf relinquished control. Devon shifted back to his human form, naked on the sidewalk. Store owners along the street yelled at him to hurry up, with someone tossing a pair of mechanic's overalls at him. Devon slid his legs into them, diving into the car just as Drew started it. He'd barely managed to close the door before his friend took off. Devon hissed and looked down at the deep cut on his shoulder. He guessed the fucker had managed to get one shot off. Shit, two, he thought as he looked down at the angry furrow across his side. This one didn't get deep enough, but he could feel the burn of silver.

He grit his teeth and waited for his wolf to heal it. If Keisha found out he'd been hurt, she would have his ass, especially since he told her that he was finally done with the shit.

Drew looked back and cursed. "I don't think those motherfuckers were from the West side."

Devon turned in his seat and saw the blue lights of city police cars behind them, stopping at the location they'd just vacated.

"We'll be straight, ain't nobody on the street talking," Drew told him.

Devon grunted because he knew that for a fact. The West side loved him and would be mum in the face of the police.

"Shit getting hectic, D," Drew said grimly.

"Can't be on top without somebody coming to eat off your plate," he told his friend. It was something Mr. D had told them all years ago. "You 'bout to be on the top now, baby. Gotta watch how you move."

Drew sucked his teeth. "They weren't there for me. They aimed straight for you." He swung around the corner and then slowed to the speed limit.

"They won't be the only ones. You scared?" Devon inspected his wound again, frowning at the deep red of the wound.

"Fuck nah," Drew said, swinging around another corner.

Devon cursed as his shoulder hit the window. "Slow this shit down, man, ain't nobody after us now."

Drew sighed but lifted his foot from the gas. "You think this got to do with you leaving the game?"

Devon thought back to how well-coordinated the attack was. "Nah, this got everything to do with Declan going after the Ruling Three position."

Drew stared at him before shaking his head. "Shit, you know we on what you on."

Devon chuckled and rested his head back. "Just take me home. Gotta hide this shit from my mate." Hell, and his brother for that matter. Declan would be cussing him up and down if he found out that someone had been shooting at him yet again.

Drew snickered but did as he asked. Devon cursed as they pulled up to his house and he saw Keisha's car. Fuck! She would give him hell.

"You good to get in the house?" He shot his friend a glare, to which Drew laughed. "Shit, I'm just saying."

Devon swallowed a groan as he stepped from the car. He would be sore as shit once the wounds healed, but even though none of the bullets were inside his body, he could feel the silver poison working through his system. Even as he headed toward the front door, his vision was swimming. The arrogance he'd felt minutes ago was waning as he clumsily put in the code.

KEISHA

Keisha paced the kitchen, unsure what to do. Her wolf was restless and pacing beneath her skin. She'd left work early because the animal wouldn't allow her to concentrate, only to get home and find the house empty. Not that she expected Devon to tell her his moves, but in the month that she'd been living with him, she could count on him being home at a certain time. He never complained about her working too much, only setting his foot down when she tired herself out.

Despite the fact that she gave him a hard time about it, she loved the way he took care of her. Sometimes he babied her, and sometimes he was on her ass.

Devon not being home had given her the idea to cook for him for once. She could hear her mother's voice in her head telling her to make sure her man felt appreciated, so that had been her plan. She teased him about being a househusband, but one look in his workshop told her that he didn't just sit around all day waiting on her to get home.

Thirty minutes ago, she'd been minding her business and humming along to music as she cooked when her heart had started thumping. Alarm and fury had slammed into her from Devon's side of the bond. Some of it dimmed, but echoes of it still filled her with anxiety. *What was going on?* Pain radiated through her, and she gasped.

She dialed Devon with shaky hands, her stomach turning when he didn't answer. He was actively trying to hide his emotions along their bond, but her wolf wasn't having it. She dialed him over and over, hanging up when the voicemail picked up and trying again. Why wasn't he answering? In between her calls to him, she was silencing calls from her cousins. That told her everything she needed to know.

Something had happened to Devon.

The fact that he wasn't answering his phone had her frantic. Tears burned her eyes; the only thing reassuring her was that she could still feel him alive along their bond. He was doing his best to hide his pain, but she could feel it.

Hearing the front door open had her frowning and picking up the knife she'd been cutting vegetables with. Devon usually came in through the garage. She headed toward the front of the house and gasped when she saw him. There was blood on the overalls he wore that were big and too small at the same time. He hadn't pulled it over his shoulders, instead tying the top around his waist. The pants were baggy, but the inseam too short.

Her heart thundered. "What happened?" She dropped the knife and rushed to him. "You weren't answering your phone."

Devon looked at her guiltily. "You're home early." It didn't answer her question.

His words were slurred, and panic had her scurrying after him as he headed upstairs. Keisha followed him into their bedroom. He went straight for the bathroom and stripped. She hurried to his side and helped him out of the pants.

"You're not answering my question. What are you hiding? Where are you hurt?" She hissed when she saw the furrow across his shoulder and rib cage.

It was from a gunshot. Her stomach dipped. His animal was trying to heal it, but the skin was still puckered and inflamed. Fur sprouted along his arms and back as his wolf fought to get free.

"You were shot?!" She couldn't help the way her voice rose. "Devon, you said you were done with this shit."

"Baby girl, I…my animal is too rough right now for me to be arguing with you," he slurred, leaning heavily on the bathroom counter.

She sucked her teeth and felt the wound. It was hot to the touch. They'd used silver. Her heart thudded.

"I'm calling mama."

"Key—" he called out, but she was already running downstairs to her cell phone.

Patrice was a retired nurse practitioner and would know what to do about possible silver poisoning. Her mother answered, and she could hardly catch her breath.

"What's wrong, baby?" Her mother's voice was calm, which helped Keisha keep it together.

"Devon was shot with silver."

"Okay, I was headed over to see you anyways, so I'm close," her mother said. "I'll be there shortly."

Just like that, Keisha's nerves settled, and though her hands still shook, she could feel her body calming. She paced the foyer of the house until the doorbell rang. She helped her mother inside, grabbing the medical supply bag Patrice always carried with her. She mostly used it when she did rounds at the local shelters, but she kept it in her car for emergencies.

Devon was leaning over the sink, his breathing labored when she got back to the bathroom. Her wolf whined, fur rippling down her arms as she lost control of the animal.

"Mama's here," she told him, wrapping a towel around his waist. "In here, mama!"

She knew that getting him back into the bathroom would be impossible if he went down on the bed, and part of the treatment for silver was to wash the wound well. Instead of guiding him into their room, she called her mother into the bathroom.

Patrice stepped in, moving Keisha aside, humming in disapproval.

"I'm fine, mama," he managed to breathe out.

Her mother sucked her teeth and laid out her supplies. Devon cursed as Patrice pressed into both wounds, examining them.

"You need to wash these out. Keisha, run a bath and add this," Patrice ordered, handing her daughter a small sachet.

Keisha did as she was told, her hands shaking.

"Didn't you tell my daughter that you were done with this shit?"

"I wasn't even in the hood, ma. This shit was done by a whole team," he gritted out.

Patrice's eyebrows winged high. "Cyrus?"

He nodded. "That's my guess."

She sighed. "I told you the game you and Declan entered had a different set of rules."

"The rules seem to be the same to me, mama. They buss, we buss back." His attempt at a joke failed as he hissed out in pain.

Patrice shook her head, dabbing at his wound. "I thought I was done with this when Leland passed."

Keisha froze, her spine stiffening at her mother's words. Devon shot a glance at her, his eyes pleading with her not to lose her shit, but it was way too late for that. Her body trembled as adrenaline and anxiety mixed within her, leaving her nauseous.

"I'm being as careful as I can," he told both women.

Keisha shuddered. It wasn't as though her job with Silas wasn't dangerous also, but this... She took a shaky breath.

"We just talked about you moving around by yourself."

"I wasn't alone, shawty. Drew was with me," he argued.

He groaned as her mother shot him up with medicine. Keisha growled as his pain broadcasted down their bond. It truly communicated his waning strength by the simple fact that he could no longer hide it from her. Once her mother was done, she went to him, helping him across the bathroom to the tub. Patrice left them alone.

Devon lifted her chin and brought her face up to his. "I'm fine, love."

"You told me you were out."

"Key, this wasn't no street shit. The people that ran down on me ain't have nothing to do with my lifestyle."

She nodded, and from the frown that marred his face, he knew she didn't believe him.

"Key," he said softly.

"I don't know if I can do this, Devon. Worrying about whether or not you're coming home. I don't..." She looked toward the door. They could both hear her mother moving around on the other side. "I can't live like she did," she whispered.

"I'm not on that, love. You've been around the Motsi enough to know how they move. Shit, at least the streets got a code. Them motherfuckers in the Motsi don't abide by shit."

He leaned his head back, his pain radiating down their bond, and she felt like shit for dumping on him while he was hurt.

"Don't give up on us," he said after a moment.

She hated the tears that dropped. She wanted to hide it all from him and take the moment alone. Her mother and father had a tacit agreement that he would keep his street shit away from them, but she would never forget the many nights her mother paced the floor, waiting on Leland to come home safely.

Devon dropped light kisses across her face. "It won't be for long, Key, I swear."

She shook her head. "I see the way Councilman Knight moves around, security constantly on watch. Is that the life you want for us?"

"I'm not leaving my brother to this shit by himself. Don't ask me to do that." He stepped back to lean on the bathroom counter, leaving her bereft of his warmth.

She swiped at the tears falling from her eyes, unable to hide them. She didn't know how to be okay with the fact that they would be risking the rest of their lives for this shit.

"Get in the tub, Devon," she ordered. "Are you hungry?" It didn't matter if he was or not. He would need food to get his strength back.

He sighed as he settled into the hot water. "Key."

She held up her hand. "Let me just... I need some air. Will you be okay in here alone for a few minutes?"

He nodded, studying her face. She stepped from him and left the bathroom.

Her mother was waiting for her on the other side of the door.

"Not now, mama," she whispered as she passed the woman.

She raced down the stairs and out the door, sucking in the humid air outside. Could she do this with him? She shook her head. Was there a choice? Her wolf told her no, and Keisha knew that she would be foolish to give up her mating because of her fear. She sighed deeply when the patio door opened behind her.

"Mama," she said.

Patrice held up a hand to stall her argument. "I know you don't want to hear it, baby, but I understand what you're going through."

She turned her tear-filled gaze to her mother to hear her out.

"At least this is for all of us. You know how the West side is suffering beneath Cyrus's rule. Your father was chasing money and street fame. Leland and Devon are not the same."

She nodded, understanding that. Her mother pulled her into her arms, and the sobs she'd been trapping in her chest escaped.

"I don't want to lose him," she cried.

"Then go to him." Her mother pulled back and cupped her cheeks, her thumb swiping at her tears. "Enjoy the moments of stillness, the in-betweens. You won't get but so many, KeKe. Take care of him the way he takes care of you because even without all this, tomorrow is never promised to us. God forbid the worst happened. Do you want to live with what you missed or be able to wrap yourself in the memories the two of you had while he's here?"

She nodded and hugged her mother tight. "I love you."

"I love you. Now, go tend to your mate, and I'll finish the dinner you started."

"You don't have to do that, mama," Keisha protested.

"I was coming over here to give my son a break from the kitchen anyway," she teased.

Keisha let out a watery laugh.

"Go. Make sure he rests because even with the antibiotics, his animal will be fighting with that silver."

She sucked in a cleansing breath and left her mother. When she got to the bathroom he was laid back in the tub, his eyes closed.

"Don't fall asleep in there. I can't carry you," she said softly.

His eyes opened and his dark gaze saw right through her calm demeanor. His wolf was staring at her through his eyes, the animal alert though still feral from pain. She kneeled next to the tub and lifted the loofah. They were silent as she bathed him. She could feel the heat from his wound every time she touched it. His breathing was getting more erratic as he lay in the water. Through their bond, she could feel his wolf battling to heal him.

"Out, my love," she told him.

He stood, still not saying a word. He was quiet while she dried him, leading him to their bedroom. She was lotioning his legs when he cupped her chin.

"We good?"

She lifted and kissed him. "I can't help my reaction. I'm scared for you."

He deepened the kiss until she was dizzy with need for air. Only then did he pull back.

"Mama is worried about fever, so lay down. I'll bring dinner to you. She's going to stay the night to make sure you're okay."

He nuzzled the side of her face and nodded. She carefully bandaged his wounds. It was up to his animal to do the rest.

"Do you need anything while I'm downstairs?"

He shook his head, and Keisha passed him her phone. It was still ringing with her cousins' messages, but his brother had called twice. She would worry about her family later.

"Your brother has been calling."

The phone rang in his hand. "I'm good, Dec," he said in greeting. "I lost my phone in the shift."

Keisha left the room to give him his privacy.

25...

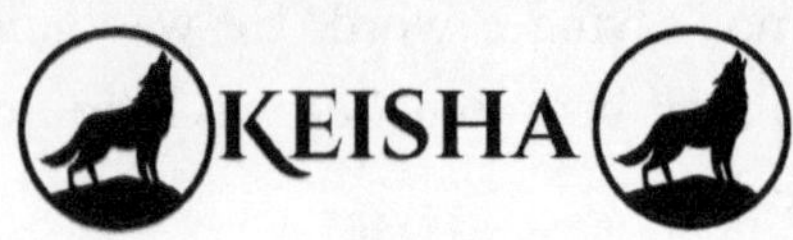

Keisha fought not to curse at the fact that their front doorbell was ringing at nine in the morning. Normally, she would be up anyway, but today she was dragging. Last night, dealing with a feverish Devon had her whole body exhausted. He'd shifted some time after midnight, roaming the house in his wolf form. By the time she found him, he'd been rooting around in the kitchen for something to eat. Keisha fed him from the steak she'd left out for this specific reason.

She'd chopped pieces of the raw meat and stored it in the fridge after Patrice warned her that his animal would be looking for it. Keisha had just been happy that the animal hadn't wanted to hunt for his food. She would've been too tired to fight her own wolf, and the animal would've followed its mate without a question. They'd fallen asleep in the living room with him in his wolf form still, his head in her lap. But this morning, she'd woken up in their bedroom, not even sure how she'd gotten there.

The smell of breakfast had woken her, and after making sure Devon's temperature was down some more, she'd left their bed. He was in his human form, so that was a good sign. She'd intended to head to the kitchen, but the doorbell had diverted her. She frowned in surprise at the pretty woman and child on her doorstep. Dressed in tight jeans and a cropped sweater, the curvy woman was shorter than Keisha and...familiar.

"Tangie, right? You were a couple of years ahead of me in school," Keisha said in lieu of a greeting. "What are you doing here?"

"I heard what happened to Devon and I wanted to check on him," Tangie rushed out. She shot a look to the kid, who had his head down. "Is he alright?" she whispered.

It was then that Keisha remembered Devon mentioning the other woman. They were friends. He'd even mentioned doing time for her. At the time, she'd kept her jealousy to herself, but now that they were mated, even seeing how beautiful Tangie was, her animal felt secure.

She stepped back. "Come, you can check on him yourself."

Tangie darted inside, the kid in tow. Keisha shut the door but then heard the sound of dishes crashing to the floor. Rushing to the kitchen, she frowned as she saw her mother's ashen face.

"What happened?" She moved to Patrice's side, bending to pick up the broken plate.

"Uncle D lives here?" the kid finally said. The nine- or ten-year-old turned in a circle to observe the house.

It was when he turned back to her that Keisha was punched in the gut. It was as if she was looking at a mini version of her father and herself. How was this possible?

"Mom," she managed to strangle out, straightening her body, dropping the piece of plate she'd picked up.

Devon carefully made his way down the stairs, wincing a little as he reached the last few steps. "What's going on?"

"Uncle D?" The little boy rushed to Devon.

Devon smiled. "Theo?" He leaned down and hugged the kid. "Let me finally get a look at you. It's different in person than on the phone."

"Mom showed me pictures of you," Theo said, holding him tight.

Keisha didn't have to ask if Devon knew because the shocked look on his face when he stepped back to look at the child said it all. He frowned and looked between the kid and Keisha. It clicked a moment later, and his gaze shot to her mother. There was devastation on his face, and she could feel it down their mating bond. Devon looked at his friend with a question in his gaze.

The front door opened and his brother swaggered in. "What's up, peoples? Ms. P, it smells amaz—" His words cut off when he saw

Tangie. Declan looked around at everyone, his brows bunched. "What's going on?"

"Theo, my brother is going to show you the beach in the back while I talk to your mother." Devon managed to keep his tone neutral.

Declan's eyes widened when Theo turned around to face him. "Oh, fu—" He cleared his throat. "Fudge. Yeah, I can do that."

The four remaining adults stood around in shocked silence as Declan escorted Theo from the room. It wasn't until the patio doors slid shut that Devon spoke.

"That's Leland's kid?" he snapped.

His question jarred Keisha out of her trance, and all at once, all the blood rushed to her head and she felt faint.

Tangie looked between Keisha and her mother. "We can talk about this later. I just came to check on you."

"Now. We should talk now," Patrice demanded.

Keisha had never heard her mother's voice so sharp and hard. Tangie shuffled foot to foot, obviously nervous.

"I didn't mean for you to find out this way, Ms. Patrice," Tangie whispered.

"You came to my house and smiled in my face. You and that Motsi kid. Marcus something," Patrice said, her eyes boring into Tangie.

Devon held up his hand. "Hold on. I need to sit down."

Keisha rushed to his side. "You're still feverish, babe," she muttered, happy to have something else to focus on. "You need to be laying down."

"Explain this, Tangie." Devon ignored Keisha's fussing but pulled her close to him. Hurt was painted on his face, the wrinkle on his forehead broadcasting his feelings. "You lied right to my face."

"Devon." Tangie headed toward him, but Keisha whipped around.

"You can say what you gotta say from there." Her wolf would lose her shit if that woman stepped any closer to her injured mate.

"Marcus Cartwright was hanging out with Leland?" He looked at Ms. Patrice for the answer. "Leland was supplying him?"

Patrice shrugged. "I didn't... You know I didn't involve myself in that business," she told Devon.

Tangie looked away. "You were never supposed to be caught up in it. Marcus swore it. It's why I introduced him to Leland."

Keisha felt sick to her stomach. Always in tune with her, Devon tightened his hold, his hand rubbing down her back.

"He needed money. Councilman Booth had slaughtered his whole family and he wanted that seat back," Tangie started to explain.

"And he needed a dispensable army. Leland was going to help him with that too?" Devon asked.

Tangie nodded.

Devon put a hand on his head. "So, you knew the drugs were in the car?"

"I'm so sorry, Devon," she whispered.

"If Marcus isn't your kid's father, then why were you helping him?" Devon gritted out.

Guilt once again transformed her façade. "He promised me a place at his side."

Devon growled low, angry. "You betrayed me for an imaginary seat at a table? I did a bid so that your child wouldn't be born behind bars, and you couldn't find it in yourself to tell me the truth at any point?"

"I didn't want to lose you," she said softly. "At first it was guilt, but I really started to have feelings for you the more we talked."

It was Keisha who growled this time, her animal slamming against her defenses. Her claws slid from behind her nails, the temptation to rake them across the other woman's face enough to have her hands shaking.

"You knew Cyrus would come after anyone aiming for his seat and you kept it from me? Leland was killed because he was helping that kid. You knew that and ain't said shit?" His wolf was furious, the sting of it electrifying their bond. "Did Drew know?"

"What do you mean?"

"Oh my fucking God," he said before slamming his hand down on the table. Keisha and her mother both flinched at the violent sound.

"Did he fucking know about Marcus?"

"Leland asked for his help so that he could keep you out of it," Tangie finally answered.

"I need to leave," Patrice said faintly.

"Mama, no." Keisha left Devon's side and helped her mother into a chair.

"You need to go," Keisha told Tangie. "Get the fuck out of my house."

"Devon." Tangie took a step toward him. "If you'll let me explain..."

He stood and turned his back to her, heading down the hallway without saying another word to her. Keisha hurried to get her mother some water, completely ignoring the other woman's presence. There was nothing but violence within her at the moment, and if she had to acknowledge that female...

Finally getting the hint, Tangie headed out the back door to get her child. Keisha hoped they went around the side of the house because she would lose it if that bitch came back in.

"Mama, I'm going to make you some tea."

"I knew about the other women. I overlooked it because he was my mate and I didn't want to fight. I hate fighting," Patrice said softly. "But a child..."

"I'm so sorry, mama." Her throat was constricted.

Keisha stood in the kitchen, frozen in indecision. She needed to clean up the shards of ceramic, she wanted to comfort her mother and mate, but she couldn't make her body do any of it. Standing stock still in the middle of the kitchen was the most she could manage.

"He's your brother," Patrice said after a moment, tears sliding down her face.

Oh God, she had a little brother. But she could deal with that later. Not now.

"I need to take care of you and Devon. I'm not there yet."

"He's innocent in all this."

"Mama, please!" she snapped, immediately sorry.

"I need to go home," Patrice said, standing.

Anger overrode all her good sense. "So you can wallow in the place where he constantly disrespected you?"

"Watch your tone, little girl."

Keisha took a deep, shaky breath. "I'm sorry, you're right. But mama, please. Let me take care of you today, and then tomorrow…"

Patrice sighed. "I guess tomorrow, we can deal with the hard parts."

Keisha nodded. It was what her mother always did when it came to trouble. She ignored it until she could work up the courage to handle the hard parts. It was the reason Keisha found herself planning her father's funeral alone. She reached through her mating bond and sent soothing energy to her mate. She could feel Devon's turmoil.

Declan came in, and she jumped.

"I didn't mean to startle you. Where is he?"

"Probably his workshop," she said softly.

Declan nodded and headed to his brother. That was one problem solved. A heavy weight filled her, her chest tight with anxiety as the full scale of what had happened registered. She'd known only a third of what her mother had been dealing with over her father. Patrice had kept his secrets, and Keisha realized she'd judged her mother so harshly because of the parts she'd not been privy to. Taking the broom out of the pantry, she handled the easiest task first. It wasn't lost on her that Patrice was in as many pieces as the plate.

After she cleaned up the mess, she pulled out her phone and hit the group chat. This wasn't something she could handle alone.

26...

After the weekend he'd had, Devon figured it was time to take his mate out of town. Not only had he been shot on Thursday, but Tangie coming over the next day had damn near blown up his life. He'd looked up to Leland, believing the family man persona he'd given to the world. To know that he was not only cheating on Ms. Patrice but doing so with a girl damn near the same age as his daughter... How had he missed a personality flaw like that?

He prided himself on being able to read and see through the bullshit, but he'd missed the biggest predator in his life. How many other young girls had his mentor preyed on? And how had he missed those signs? At the time, Devon had his head down, his instincts focused solely on survival for him and his sibling, but...still...

All weekend, his house had been filled with Keisha's family, her aunt and cousins hunkering down to love on her mother in her time of need. It was a beautiful thing to witness. He thought for sure it would be an 'I hate men' fest, but the women had made sure he was recovering well while they went about their business.

How could he not be in love with his mate and her family?

Monday dawned with him feeling significantly better and his mate ready to get back to her schedule as usual. That woman worked way too damn hard. He knew convincing her to go away for a trip would be difficult. But once he got his brother that council seat, he was taking his mate out of the country, even if he had to tie her to the top of the plane.

He entered the kitchen to find her at the stove, dressed for work but still making him breakfast. He snuggled up to her back, wrapping his arms around her waist. The sleeveless navy dress she wore hugged her curvy figure, the discreet vee at the neck giving him a tease of her cleavage.

Shawty looked fine as fuck.

"You making me breakfast?" He nuzzled against the back of her neck.

Her hair was tied up into a high bun, leaving the nape exposed. He kissed her softly, rubbing his cheek against her skin.

"Don't mess up my hair," she fussed. "You have to take your last dose of antibiotics with food, so I want to make sure you do that before I leave."

He sighed when his doorbell rang. He would be good on guests for a little while. He kissed Keisha's temple and hurried to the front door. Julian stood on his front stoop, a laptop tucked beneath his arms.

"This shit fly," Julian commented, entering before Devon could invite him in. "I need to see if my baby wants something by the water."

"Why you here so early?" Devon asked.

"Shouldn't you be laying down?" Julian said instead of answering, following Devon into the kitchen.

"Thank you! I tried to tell him that," Keisha said from the stove. "Good morning, Jules."

"Morning, Keisha."

Devon grunted, ignoring them both.

"Declan's mad as hell," Julian told him. "He called me early this morning about the shooting."

"He'll be alright," Devon murmured, sitting at the island. "It's been three days."

Julian sat next to him and placed his laptop on the counter. "You want me to wait to tell you what I found out?"

Devon looked at Keisha and debated. She was his mate and would need to know about all aspects of his life. If he was going to be fully in this shit with Declan, then she needed to be riding with him.

"You can talk in front of my mate," he said, and Jules smiled wide. "Man, gone head."

"I ain't even say anything," Julian joked. "Anyway. Remember you asked me to look over that shit with Marcus Cartwright?"

"Fuck, don't even remind me." Devon wiped his hand down his face.

"What happened?" Julian asked as he maneuvered through files on his laptop.

He broke down what Tangie had told them yesterday and Julian whistled.

"Then what I got on that front is old news."

"Wait, people knew about him and Tangie?"

Julian shrugged before shooting a glance toward Keisha. "I don't know about everyone, but there were some rumors about Leland and a couple different girls that even I hadn't heard. But...back to Marcus. Some people in the Motsi are saying that he'd tried to take back his father's seat and lost his life over it. But we talked about that the other day at the office."

Devon shook his head. Ten years of his life gone for some shit he wasn't even involved in.

"Since that's out the way, let's talk about the attempts on you." Julian changed the subject. "So...Drew."

Devon frowned. "'What about Drew?"

"Follow me for a second. Leland was supplying Marcus, that's clear from what Tangie told y'all. But Leland turned the whole trade over to you, and presumably, you would know if a big chunk of your inventory was going missing, right?"

"Fucking right."

He opened his mouth to say something else but closed it because he understood what Julian was saying. At the time, Devon had been in charge for less than a year. Leland had promoted Drew to inventory, and Devon trusted both his friend and his mentor. So, if a couple of small keys had gone missing here or there, he would've trusted Drew to figure it out.

Julian continued. "Only thing I could figure out was that your boy was skimming. Back then it was drugs, but he's moved on to money these days. But that's not really...I mean, you're out, so who cares if he's stealing his own money?"

"Shit, I care. If he skimming, then the people under him not getting what they should," Devon protested as his anger spiked.

"Okay, fair." Julian moved through some screens and turned his laptop to face Devon. "So, anyway, I checked Councilman Booth's phone records for the time you got locked up — and that shit was hard as hell, by the way."

Devon's eyes skimmed over the records, and he cursed as he recognized phone numbers that he'd called for years while he was locked up. Drew went through a lot of burners but because he couldn't leave a trail, Devon never added the numbers as contacts. He had to dial them shits by hand every time he talked to Drew, so he recognized a good number of them.

"Drew was talking to Cyrus?"

"With the information Tangie added, my guess is he saw an opportunity to move up, so to speak. He could get rid of you and Leland."

Devon shook his head. "Nah, Drew don't move like that."

Julian swiped another screen. These phone records were more recent. The two men were still talking. Devon cursed. Julian then pulled up surveillance video from the day of the shooting and tapped on a file labeled for Thursday evening. Devon shook his head, already knowing what his friend was about to show him.

"He could've been caught in the crossfire," he said as he tried to reconcile the information he was seeing.

Julian shook his head and hit play. They were talking to shop owners, then Drew pulled out his phone and made a call. He fast-forwarded it twenty minutes to the time when the car pulled up and the men got out. They both watched as Drew stood back while the men came directly at Devon. He cursed. Drew was dead just as soon as he caught up with him.

Keisha set a plate in front of him and the almost-empty pill bottle. Her hands were shaking, but he didn't sense fear from her.

"Just move carefully," she said as she placed a plate down in front of Julian.

"I won't do anything impulsive," he promised.

She sighed before shaking her head. "I'm going into work." She walked to his side of the island and kissed his cheek.

"You not eating?" He pulled her into his chest.

"I can't right now. I'll grab something at the office, promise," she told him.

He kissed her deeply. "You finna start stressing over me, and I need you not to do that."

She snorted. "Yeah, I'll let my anxiety know that."

He nuzzled her cheek. His wolf rubbed against hers, the animal's apprehension translating across their bond.

"I'm not going nowhere, love."

She kissed him. "Just be careful, and get someone else to be around you. Clearly Drew was a terrible choice for backup."

He laughed and nodded. "Text me when you get in."

"You sure you don't need me to stay?" She bit her lip, her gaze tracing his face.

"I'll be fine," he told her for the fiftieth time since they woke up this morning.

"Aye, why the fuck you ain't in bed?" Declan demanded as he came into the front door without knocking.

Devon pointed his hand toward his brother in a 'see' motion.

"Get him, Dec," Keisha said on her way out, stopping to nuzzle against Declan's cheek in greeting.

"You supposed to be on my side, Key," Devon called out.

"Bye, baby!" she said, leaving out the front door.

"I'm fine, Dec," he growled. "Ms. Patrice got me straight, and my wolf did the rest," he assured his brother.

"So, you did get my message?" Declan greeted Julian. "What did you find out?"

"Don't be calling my fucking phone so early in the morning," Julian said in lieu of an answer.

Declan grabbed a piece of bacon from Julian's plate. "It got you over here, didn't it?"

Julian and Devon shared a look. His brother's mouth was so reckless. He could only laugh.

"Run it down for me, please," Declan said to placate the lion.

Julian grunted but pulled up everything he'd found. Devon's leg was bouncing as his friend went over it all again, fuming over the betrayal. Hurt and fury took turns battling in his chest. Somebody would die behind playing with his life, and his old friend was first in line.

<h1 style="text-align:center">27...</h1>

"Will you be able to do it?"

It was a valid question — one Devon didn't want to think about. Could he kill one of his oldest friends? With the sting of betrayal burning through his chest, he knew with certainty that he could.

And would.

Allowing Drew to live kept a target on Devon's back and, in turn, his brother's. There was no question of a choice when it came to his brother. He would choose Declan's life over even his own. Declan looked over at him, his forehead furrowed, waiting on his answer.

"I can do it, if need be," his brother offered.

Devon sucked his teeth. "I went to jail for ten years and came back to you being a thug? Did I not tell your narrow ass to stay on the right side of the law?"

"We all we got, big brother, fuck you thought? I was gonna sit around while you made all the sacrifices for us?" Declan shook his head and turned his attention back to the house they were watching.

Devon grunted, unable to argue with that, though it hurt his heart to know he'd led his brother down this path despite his intentions. His father's last words to a six-year-old Devon had been to take care of the brother still baking in his mother's stomach, and he'd never taken it lightly. Even his grandmother had extracted the same promise, though she'd simply asked that he guide Declan to be better than their circumstances. He grunted because technically, they were in a better place financially. He wasn't sure Frida would agree with the way they'd gone about it.

"It's fine, Dev." Declan broke into his thoughts.

He ignored his brother. Devon's feelings were his own, and nothing Declan could say would remove that guilt. Devon focused his attention back to the house. According to Julian, the small bungalow-style house was in another woman's name, but Drew lived there. Devon wouldn't have believed it if he hadn't witnessed Drew pulling into the short driveway. The only thing that had stopped him and Declan from descending on the place was the children's toys scattered across the yard.

Were there kids inside? He talked to Drew damn near every day, and besides the cub he had with Claudia, his friend had made no mention of kids. It was a risk he was not willing to take, though, so he and his brother found a discreet distance to park and wait Drew out. They'd showed up at nightfall, and it was now nearing midnight. He would sit out here all night, though, if needed.

"This motherfucker got a whole family hidden out here," Declan said softly. "He ain't tell you that shit, huh?"

"You know how the game go," Devon grumbled.

For the most part, knowing where a person laid their head at night was a secret few knew. Any other time, Devon could respect it.

"Yeah, but a family? That's shady as hell. I thought you said he and Claudia was still messing around? These kids old enough to ride a bike, which means they're older than Claudia's kid with him."

Devon sucked his teeth and shot his brother a dry look. "You finna narrate the whole night?"

"Excuse the fuck out of me," Declan said, chuckling.

Devon sat up straight when the front door opened. There was finally movement. He glanced at his brother as he restarted the stolen car they were sitting in. Once they were done with it, Devon had someone lined up to chop it and get rid of the parts. There would be no trace of the vehicle.

"You sure you want to be caught up in this? You got enough on your plate as is."

"I'm on what you on," Declan snapped.

Devon chuckled at his offense. "Shit, I had to ask, ol' sensitive ass. Let's get this shit over with so I can get back to my baby."

They both watched as Drew got into a car that Devon had never seen him in. The nondescript sedan must belong to the woman inside the house. He shook his head. His friend was moving foul. He pulled out behind the car and followed him at a distance. Drew led them to the warehouse district and one of the warehouses Devon knew they used for drop-offs. He pulled off the road and turned off the lights, slowing down the car until they slid into one of the alleys in view of the building.

It was the same one where Devon had met Drew weeks ago. There was no reason Drew should be operating out of just one warehouse. He had to shake his head because when he was running shit, no one could sit anywhere near his shit without him knowing. When no one came out of the warehouse in the ten minutes they sat there, he cursed.

"Sloppy ass motherfuckers, man."

Declan looked around. "It could be a setup."

Devon grunted in agreement. "I want this shit done, though."

His phone vibrated across the dash. He sucked his teeth at the text message a moment before the back doors opened.

"I could've shot both of y'all," he said dryly as Rock and Jules slid into the car.

"We texted," was Rock's answer to that.

"I thought y'all was done with this kind of stuff when y'all mated," Declan teased.

Julian scoffed. "Yeah, right."

"How did you know he would be at this warehouse?" Devon asked.

"Unlike you, Drew don't move his counting spot around," Julian answered.

Devon shook his head. Just sloppy and arrogant. Even with Drew having a tri-council member moving for him, it reeked of laziness. It was one of the reasons Devon was promoted over Drew in the first place. His friend always wanted easy.

"What we doing?" Rock asked, loading a clip into his Glock.

Devon sighed and pulled his heat from under the seat. "Gon' clear that bitch out."

As they exited the car, a black truck down the road opened its doors and four more goons stepped out.

"That's you?" Jules asked, his eyebrows high.

"You know how I move," Devon told him.

"You trust them?" Rocco asked, keeping his eyes on them.

"Man, you know my fucking name," he muttered.

They rolled up onto the warehouse, finding the perimeter empty. The buildings were a mix of brick and steel, the alleys between narrow and dark. There were some small factories housed in the district; even the one where their father had lost his life was close. Two or three blocks up, the area was slowly being cleaned up, but these warehouses in the back were largely left alone. The streetlights were broken if they were on at all. It was the perfect place to hide.

Everything about it screamed setup, but Devon wasn't backing down. Staring at the lock on the door, Devon sighed. He'd watched Drew put in the code the last time he was here, and he was almost certain it hadn't changed. Dialing in the six-digit code, he shook his head when the shit worked. Drew's sloppiness would be his demise.

Lazy motherfuckers, man.

They entered the warehouse, this particular one two floors, with the first floor open from front to back. A metal railing ringed the second floor where there were multiple offices. When Devon ran the game, those offices were used for various meetings, and as counting rooms when it suited. As Rocco said, he changed locations often. From a quick glance, Drew had the place empty. The shelves that were full of work the last time he'd come through were now cleared out. So were the workers.

In the middle of the floor were three tables; one was covered with money, the other two weapons. Drew and a high-level official from Cyrus's cabinet sat at the table with a money counter buzzing between them. Devon recognized the man from the fundraiser. Dallas had made it a point to identify all of Cyrus's hierarchy to Devon and his brother as he introduced them to others in the Motsi.

There were three steely-eyed shifters standing behind Drew, AKs across their chests as the money machine on the table rumbled in use. Rock let off shots, and Devon could only chuckle as the three guards went down one after the other. Rocco moved so fast that none of the men had a chance to react. It was down to just Drew and the official. Neither of the men flinched when their guards hit the ground.

Points for them.

But Devon wasn't surprised. Drew had never been pussy, so it was so strange to him that he would be disloyal after all this time. Since their presence was now known, Devon moved from the shadows, his brother at his back.

"Tell me something, Drew," he said to his friend.

Drew sat back in the chair and crossed his arms over his chest. "The game is the game, Dev. Like you said, people always trying to eat off your plate."

"So loyalty ain't mean shit to you?"

"I'm loyal to my fucking self!" Drew slapped his chest.

"Bet," Devon said.

His rage boiled over and his body expanded as his wolf took over, forcing his shift. His clothes were in shreds as his animal jumped from the scraps toward Drew. His friend stood with barely enough time for his own wolf to burst from him before Devon was on him. Devon's wolf was nearly twice the size of Drew's, the animal damn near feral after years of confinement in prison. He slammed into Drew, the sound of their bodies colliding echoing throughout the building. The two of them went at it, his wolf tearing through someone he'd considered a friend.

Drew was a scrappy fighter, his claws piercing Devon's side as his agile body twisted beneath him. Their bodies were tangled, fur flying, their primal growls filling the air. Drew was good, but he was no match for the anger coalesced within Devon's animal. Neither he nor the wolf took disloyalty lightly. In their circumstances, it meant danger to everyone important to them, and his animal wouldn't tolerate the threat. Finally able to pin Drew down, the wolf struck a blow that meant death for his friend. His canines latched onto Drew's throat, blood flowing quickly from the grievous wound. His animal didn't let up, even when Drew's body went still beneath his paws.

Only then did the animal relent and allow Devon to change back to human. Agony was written across Drew's face. With his body bruised and bleeding, Devon stepped back, his breathing choppy as he stared down at the bloody body of one of his oldest friends. The metallic taste of blood coated his tongue, and his gums ached as his teeth receded. Memories of him and Drew flashed before him as his emotions swelled and threatened to take him off his square. They'd grown up together, made rank within Leland's gang together. Nothing could've prepared Devon for this outcome.

"I would've given you anything. You didn't have to go behind my back," Devon said, the anger slowly draining from his body, leaving only sadness in its wake.

"You don't know how bad it got out here, man," Drew managed to whisper.

As the life bled from Drew's body, Devon couldn't help the tears that flowed down his cheeks. "See you in hell," he told his friend as he took his final breath.

It pained him both physically and emotionally. His wolf howled in anguish and grief, his chest constricted. He turned to Cyrus's adviser and eyed the older man.

"We coming for your shit," he warned him.

The older man smirked. "Cyrus is not without his own resources." He nodded toward Drew's dead body. "There is no shortage of greedy bodies willing to lay down for a few dollars."

"Is that right?" Declan said softly, stepping next to his brother. He shot the man in his shoulder, the male's arm falling useless to his side. "I'ma go through every step of your hierarchy, and I'ma lay down everybody who used our people as fodder."

Declan shot again, this time in the male's thigh. The man yelled out, going down to his knees, his face registering that he wasn't leaving the warehouse alive.

"I was going to leave you to carry a message back to Cyrus, but instead, I think your body will convey the statement better." Declan's next shot was a headshot, killing the older shifter.

Devon sighed in exhaustion. "I was supposed to keep you out of shit like this."

Declan pointed to Drew. "See what keeping me out did? Got some pussy ass ho watching your back." He spit on Drew's body and nodded toward the door. "Bring your naked ass on. It's some clothes in the car."

Rocco snickered.

"See how sickening he done got?" Julian complained, handing Devon the bag of money Drew had been counting. "Be all at my house, eating my food and shit."

They busted out laughing, the release of it clearing some of the adrenaline still spiking his blood.

"You gotta suck that up. He's always been protective of Deena," Rock told their friend, smiling.

Devon looked around as the crew he'd called started cleaning up. He dropped the duffel filled with cash on the table, nodding toward the crew so they knew the contents were theirs to split. They paused to acknowledge it before going back to their work. Devon knew that by the morning, there would be no trace of anything happening in the warehouse. Bypassing the car they'd stolen, Devon met his brother at the black pickup truck that Julian and Rocco had arrived in.

Declan passed him a bag full of gym clothes. "Dev, have one of your boys drop ol' boy off where Cyrus can find him."

"Shiiit, he might be colder than you, Dev," Rock said, getting into the truck.

He could only chuckle because a lot had clearly changed since he'd been locked up. He quickly slid on the basketball shorts, his wolf still moving restlessly around his body. The only thing that would settle the animal now was getting sight of his mate. The thought of the comfort

Key would bring him had him scurrying into the truck, anxious to be in her presence.

28...

Julian dropped them off at their vehicles in Declan's office parking lot where they'd left them, and the brothers headed to their respective cars. Devon nodded at Declan as he pulled off a few moments later, waiting until his brother rounded the corner before he went to his trunk. Changing his clothes in the empty parking lot, Devon donned a black sweatsuit and all-black sneakers. Sliding a hat over his head, he got into his car. There was one more stop he needed to make before he could make it back to his baby. The play was a lot later than he'd planned but still in place, nonetheless.

This time he didn't bother with a stolen car, wanting his target to know exactly who was paying him a visit. Ten minutes later, he pulled onto Cliff House Lane, killing the headlights. He parked down from the gate and smiled as he saw the soldiers he'd sent ahead in place. Pulling the black knit cap down onto his head, Devon swaggered to the front gate. The security guard that should've been there was replaced, Terrance smiling at him as he keyed in the code to open the gate.

"You hell, Dev," Terrance joked.

"We finna dead this shit tonight," Devon told him.

Devon jogged up the long driveway, impatience tinging his every step. The mansion looked at least three stories high, the cobblestones of the circular driveway parting in the middle for a huge stone fountain. There should've been guards around the perimeter of the house, circling the property in patrol, but his crew had gotten rid of them before he'd arrived. There would be nothing stopping him from gaining entrance.

Walking straight through the double glass doors at the front, Devon's footsteps were silent as he moved through the mansion, shaking his head at all the excess while people on the West side starved. His brother would change all that, and Devon couldn't wait to help him. The ceilings were sky-high with marble floors stretching throughout the length of the foyer and down several hallways. A crystal chandelier reflected moonlight from the floor-to-ceiling windows, casting prisms across the cold, sterile interior.

He was thankful that he'd been able to obtain a floor plan of this mausoleum because he couldn't imagine trying to find his target in here. Devon made his way upstairs and into the bedroom, having already memorized its location. The room was pitch-black, two bodies in the California King-sized bed. He stood over the bed and waited.

It didn't take long for Cyrus to startle awake. He had to give him points for his heart because there was no fear in the older wolf's eyes when he noticed Devon in his room. Cyrus's gaze went to his bedside table and the gun that Devon had already emptied of bullets.

"My brother coming for your spot, whether you take me out or not."

Cyrus frowned and looked to his sleeping wife.

"Don't even worry about her. She'll be out for a while."

The older man sat up and shook his mate. "What did you do?"

"Same shit I did to all the staff in this place. I wanted time for us to have this conversation uninterrupted."

"You came to send me a warning? For what? Your brother has already called the challenge."

"I know you had Leland killed. The only reason I haven't scattered your brain across your pillow is because I don't want it coming back on my brother, but trust, your day is coming." Devon got pissed all over again.

"He should've kept his nose out of Motsi business. The same with your brother."

Devon waved his hand to dismiss that bullshit. "I came to tell you that the next time you send someone after me on some coward shit, I'm taking out everyone around you, starting with that pretty lady next to you."

"That had nothing to do with me. Your so-called friend wanted your spot."

Devon shrugged because that could be true, but it was inconsequential to why he was here. He took out the burner phone in his pocket. "So, is this not your man meeting with Drew?"

Cyrus hissed at the picture of the male's dead body next to Drew's. Erasing the picture, Devon put the burner phone back in his pocket.

"You came to brag? Your brother will never last in my seat," Cyrus promised, anger raising his wolf.

"Oh, yeah? We'll see, won't we?" Devon said with a smirk. "Now, you can do this shit the way it's laid out in y'all's bullshit ass laws, or we can get into some gangsta shit. Either way you can be touched. Declan is of a mind to do it the right way, but that can be changed at any moment."

Devon made his way back to the door. "Stay safe out here," he told the man, giving him back the same words Cyrus had given them at the fundraiser.

He exited the house the same way he came in, knowing his team had all the cameras on the property disabled. Maybe his threat would work, maybe it wouldn't. Either way, Devon was done with it. Terrance met him at the gate.

"Walk with me," he told his friend.

Terrance walked him to the car, his curious eyes scanning Devon's face.

"Drew's gone."

There was no surprise in Terrance's eyes.

"You knew what he was up to?"

"Shit got bad, man. But you was backing him and wasn't nobody moving against you." Terrance's tone was matter-of-fact.

"You got a crew?" Devon asked, mindful of his next words.

He knew Terrance from around the way. He'd slowly been making his way up the ranks when Leland had turned everything over to Devon. Everything Devon knew about the male told him that he was trustworthy. Terrance was a relative of Leland's, and in turn, Keisha's. Devon hoped that would be enough to count on his loyalty.

"Been building one since Drew started making shady moves," Terrance admitted.

"Why you ain't come to me, man? We in this shit just as deep."

"Yeah, but that was your boy. Sometimes friendships be trumping the money."

Devon scoffed. "That ain't never the case with me," he told him. Devon wiped a hand down his face. "So, you think you can do this?"

"I just been waiting on an opening. You give me the connect and it's done."

"Bet," Dev said softly. "I want loyalty in return."

"You already got that based on you dealing with the family. Your credibility has never been tied to that snake."

Devon nodded because that was fair. "I'm still around when you need shit, though."

"No doubt. Handle your business and I got the rest. With Drew gone, our people can get back to eating. When Declan takes over..." he left off, and Devon nodded.

"We'll work it out. We would never turn our backs on the West side," Devon promised him.

"Then we straight," Terrance assured him.

"I'm out then," Devon said, getting into his car.

He was ready to get back to his mate.

Keisha was singing to herself, trying to distract her mind. She didn't know if it was a good thing that Devon didn't hide anything from her. On one hand, she would worry about where he was and what he was doing, but on the other hand, a betrayal like the one her mother was dealt was not likely to happen. She shook her head because even she knew that wasn't accurate. A man could play in her face even if she was doing all the right things. Her heart and instincts told her Devon would never do that to her.

But then, she would've never thought her father would have an outside child on her mother.

When she was thirteen, she'd heard the first of many arguments her parents had had about Leland's other women. Keisha hadn't thought it possible for mates to cheat, but her father had proved that wrong. To her, it showed a severe lack of bonding with his animal. She loved Devon with her whole heart; their souls melded when they mated, to the point where she even found it uncomfortable to be around other men for too long. How, then, was her father able to push past that to not only cheat but to have a child with another woman? And were there more?

Keisha sighed and pushed the steam mop harder, her arms aching from doing the entire downstairs. Devon kept their house damn near spotless, a side effect of his nightmares. Keisha had found him up more than once cleaning when he couldn't sleep, so really, there wasn't anything for her to do other than steam the floors.

While she thought the cleaning would distract her, it had made her thoughts crystal clear, the mindless task giving her focus. All night, thoughts of her parents' mating had circled her brain. Not that it was her business, but she could never understand why her mother put up with it. She'd spent several therapy sessions over the years wondering why Patrice allowed Leland to run over her. Keisha had pushed away plenty of relationships for fear of ending up with a man just like her father. It hadn't been worth the effort.

Until she mated with Devon.

Now she understood the yearning from the animal and the soul-wrenching need for her mate. How, then, did Patrice cope with the constant betrayal? It had to feel as though a part of her body was being severed. Keisha realized that all her feelings for her mother came from a childish standpoint. In the mind of a child, everything was black or white. It had taken one glance at Devon for shades of gray to start obscuring her rigid views.

Though she'd fought with Devon about mating with him, at the end of the day, denying him hadn't been possible. It helped that he was very upfront with her. When he gave his word, she believed him. It still wouldn't stop her animal from getting active when she felt another woman encroaching on what was hers. That made her smile because besides the fact that she got to put bitches in their place, Devon's reaction to it made it fun. He acted like he felt some type of way about it, but his version of asserting his dominance included orgasms, so that would never be a deterrent.

She finished steaming the hallways and gave up cleaning. Jumping in the shower, she tried to keep her thoughts positive. It was almost two in the morning. Surely, he was done by now. She froze as she stopped the water twenty minutes later, hearing the sound of the garage door opening. Forgoing clothes, she jumped out of the shower stall, wrapping a towel around her body and rushing to the bedroom.

Keisha spotted him when she reached the top of the stairs. His body was draped in only a pair of low-slung jogging pants, its matching hoodie in his hands. They weren't the clothes he'd left in, and that reassured her more than anything. The only reason he would've had to change was if his animal had shredded through his clothes. If he was shifting, then bullets were less likely to be flying around.

Her eyes raked over the rest of his body to take him in. His chest was covered in healing scratches and bites, bruising marring his dark skin. His eyes were feral as he sought her out. They heated when he realized she was naked. Devon took the stairs two at a time, meeting her at the top. He pulled her into his arms, his chest rumbling with a low growl.

She inhaled deeply, pulling in the wild essence of his wolf. She could smell faintly the scent of gunpowder and knew that someone had been shooting around him if he wasn't the one doing it himself. She wouldn't ask, not wanting that level of detail. He lifted her into his arms, wrapping her legs around him. The towel fell, exposing her wet body. His eyes glowed gold, his power raising goosebumps along her skin.

"I missed you."

"I don't know how. You been blowing up my phone," she lied, knowing it was her sending him messages to check on him.

He chuckled darkly, scraping his teeth across her chest.

Keisha shuddered in anticipation, but her animal's need to care for him kept her on task. "Let me down so I can run you a shower."

"I can do that myself," he whispered against her lips, dropping light kisses as he walked them to their bedroom.

She smiled. "Well, according to Patrice, I gotta take care of my man."

He laughed. "You gon' leave my mama alone."

"I love that you think of her that way."

"Me and Mama locked in, you the hardheaded one taking forever."

She laughed. "You're both ridiculous."

He kissed her, his tongue swiping at her lips. She opened her mouth, eagerly sucking his tongue in. He ravished her and she enjoyed every second of it.

His eyes were hooded when he pulled back. "I love you, Key," he whispered, and her body melted.

"I love you, Devon."

"Let me shower, then I want to lay up under you," he murmured, nuzzling her cheek.

"You always up under me."

"Under you." He kissed her lips. "On top of you." He nipped her chin. "Inside of you," he said, sucking her bottom lip into his mouth. "I'm trying to be all that."

Her stomach clenched in lust and she licked her lips, using her feet to pull him into her more. His dick pressed against her center, and she shuddered as need filled her.

Shit, a quickie wouldn't hurt and could certainly be seen as taking care of her mate, she reasoned. Using her heels, she shoved down his pants, licking her lips at finding him naked underneath. Keisha moved an arm from around his neck, sliding her hand down to grip his dick.

Devon growled and set her feet down on the ground. Before she could complain, he spun her body around.

She gripped the double vanity, smiling as Devon pressed down on the middle of her back. "Arch that shit," he ordered in a dark, gravelly voice.

Keisha hurriedly obliged, closing her eyes as he slid his hardness across the folds of her sex.

"Already wet," he murmured approvingly, sliding inside. "Eyes up, mamas. I want you watching."

Keisha pried her lids apart, her stomach clenching at the naked want on Devon's face reflected in the mirror. The way his eyes blazed as he scanned her body had goosebumps rising on her skin. The stark craving that lit his eyes… Her canines dropped and her animal howled in pleasure. The need to bite him, to sink her teeth back into her mark consumed her. Standing from her position, Keisha slid off his dick and turned, bringing his head down to hers. Devon growled and lifted her to the vanity, shoving back inside. She hissed in pleasure.

"Mine." She licked across his shoulder and her mark.

Devon shuddered, his strokes speeding. Keisha moaned, scraping her teeth across his skin. She bit down, and Devon threw his head back, howling as his blood entered her mouth. They were already bonded, the mark already permanent, but it didn't stop Keisha from pushing her power into the bite. He'd called her possessive before and she would be that all day for him. Pride that he belonged to her in all ways constricted her chest. Energy flooded their bond, the strength of it spinning her head.

His dick swelled, broadcasting how close he was to release. His knot locked into place, pressing against her g-spot. It sent her up, fire burning through her bloodstream as she was pitched into an orgasm. She released his skin, drunk off the sensation of his wolf moving along their bond.

"Come for me," she demanded, feeling herself teetering right on that edge again.

Devon bit down on his own mark and that sent her careening into another powerful climax. She couldn't even scream. It took everything in her to stay conscious as euphoria stripped all sense of being from her. His body stiffened as Devon came. He hugged her tight, their bodies locked together as he filled her. She didn't know how long they stayed in their positions, but her mind floated, her thoughts hazy and lazy.

"So fucking aggressive," Devon slurred, his hand softly skimming her body.

"Don't care," she murmured, licking across his skin.

He chuckled. "No work tomorrow."

She sucked her teeth but didn't argue with the stubborn wolf. She'd already had no plans to work, but because he was being bossy, her pettiness reared its head. Her mate, knowing her so well, laughed as he lifted her, finally able to withdraw from her body.

"Don't worry, you'll be too tired to move when I'm done with you," he promised.

Liking the sound of that, Keisha smiled. "We can spend the day at the beach."

Devon had the water already started and warm when he pulled their bodies into the shower stall. "That sounds perfect. It'll be our last easy day before it all starts."

Her heart thumped, but she pushed aside her worry. She trusted Devon, and in turn, Declan. Life with him would be worth it, no matter the hardships they needed to get through to claim it. Did she want to be part of the Motsi? Not necessarily. But would she do it to support her mate and to have Devon in her life? Without a doubt.

He was worth it. They were worth it, and Keisha was ready to see what the rest of her life would look like as Devon's mate.

Epilogue...

Devon loaded the last bit of charcoal into the back of his pickup truck. He'd traded his Rover in a week ago, liking the truck better for his purposes. He needed something to haul around parts and supplies. Now that he'd backed out of the street shit permanently, he was making plans to do what pleased him. To that end, he'd signed up for classes at the HBCU the next town over for the upcoming fall season. He would get his degree in electrical engineering to see where it would take him.

It would probably feel weird going to school with a bunch of young kids, but he would do what he needed to do to give his mate the life she wanted. He liked tinkering in his workshop, and if his brother could make him money from it, all the better.

Speaking of his brother, Devon checked his watch and shook his head as Declan pulled into his driveway fifteen minutes later than what he said he would do. He pressed the button to close the garage now that he had everything he needed.

"You could've just met me at Ms. Patrice's house," he told Declan as his brother stepped out of the Mercedes with his security.

"Dang, I can't ride with my big brother?"

Devon chuckled and dapped his brother, grabbing him into a hug. They butted heads, their animals rushing forward in greeting. Ever since he was out, both he and his brother made the most of it. If Devon wasn't bothering him at work, Declan was showing up to Devon's house while Key was working. He held his brother tighter for just a moment, knowing that his challenge with Cyrus was in a couple of days. Devon cleared his throat and stepped back, refusing to allow his thoughts to go too far.

"We need to bounce, Ms. Patrice waiting on me," Devon said, heading for the front door. He opened it and leaned into the house. "Key, bring your ass!"

"Don't be rushing me!" she yelled back as she came outside. Devon took the tray of deviled eggs from her and locked the front door.

"Morning, sis," Declan greeted, grabbing the cake carrier in the fancy bag to hold it.

"Morning, Dec." Keisha nuzzled under his brother's chin, their animals greeting each other. She turned back to her man. "You and Patrice not finna get on my nerves today, Devon."

He could only smile. She was in a pair of cut-off shorts that had him ready to say fuck a family kickback.

"Aye, come here a sec, shawty," he ordered.

"Aht-aht!" Declan mushed his head. "Don't start that shit. KeKe, you gotta ride in the back. I'm not trying to watch a porn flick on the way to this barbecue."

"I'm 'bout to shoot you in the face," Devon threatened, to which Keisha and Declan both laughed at his empty threat.

He set the eggs into the back seat and helped his mate in as Declan ordered his security to trail them. His hands skimmed Keisha's thighs as she settled into the seat. Devon nuzzled in the space between her neck and shoulder, licking her skin. He nipped his mating mark, smiling as she shuddered.

"Your brother told you to behave," she simpered.

"Fuck him," he murmured, kissing her softly.

"Don't make me get violent," Declan said, getting into the passenger seat.

Keisha laughed and pushed Devon's head away. "Let's go before your mama text me again asking where we at."

He chuckled and rounded the truck. Happiness filled him, all the things in his life right where he wanted them. It took them only twenty minutes to get to her mother's house. Ms. Patrice was waiting on the porch for them as he parked in her driveway. She smiled as he walked up, pulling him into a hug.

"I know my daughter is the reason you're later than you said," she teased, nuzzling his cheek. Her panther brushed his wolf in greeting.

Keisha sucked her teeth behind him, and Devon laughed. "Her and Declan"

Patrice pulled Declan into a hug. "It's a pleasure to see you again, love."

Devon smiled as the tension in Declan's shoulders subsided. Ms. Patrice had that way about her. Just being in her presence was relaxing. He was glad that his brother felt the same way.

She pulled back from Declan. "I pulled the grill out of the garage, and there were charcoals from the last get-together."

"I got everything I need in the truck, ma. I just want to see what we're working with."

She nodded and led him to the backyard. It still looked good from where he cut the grass last week. Ms. Patrice already had the furniture he'd bought her set up in her patio. He'd strung up the lights himself when he came by the other day. She had protested him spending money on her, but he needed both women to understand that he took care of his family.

"This group eats like the carnivores they are, so I already have some meat seasoned and taken out of the deep freezer," Patrice told him as they reentered the kitchen.

Keisha was at the counter, icing the cake she'd made last night, and Declan was sitting at the kitchen table on his phone.

He wrapped his arms around her waist. "How you doing?" He could feel her nerves.

"My family is a lot," she told him. "Especially daddy's side. I don't want to overwhelm you or your wolf."

He warmed at her consideration and kissed her neck. "I'll be straight. You keep your hands to yourself and we shouldn't have no problems."

Patrice cackled, and Keisha sucked her teeth.

His phone buzzed in his pocket and he pulled it out, frowning at Tangie's name. He sent the call to voicemail like he'd been doing for the past week. He'd given his phone number to Theo directly so the kid could call if he needed something. At the end of the day, Devon had already established a relationship with the kid, and Theo was Keisha's brother. He couldn't see himself in good conscience not taking care of someone who was Leland and Keisha's family.

If and when his mate came around, he wanted to make sure there was an open line of communication for the two siblings to get to know each other. That didn't mean he would be talking to Tangie. He had life nearly exactly where he wanted it. There was no room in it for people who weren't loyal.

Keisha took a sigh of relief around hour four of the family barbecue. Her mother's backyard was packed, and so far, most people were on their best behavior. She and Declan had just finished beating ass at the spades table. He was so different than his brother. Declan was a little more easy-going than Devon, though both of them had that streak of dominance that filled the air around them. Even cousins who were quick to start shit were careful around Declan.

Sporadically, she would check on Devon at the grill, but he seemed to be fine. He was in a serious conversation with her grandfather and uncles. Laughter sounded out from there every now and then. She knew that with his brother's upcoming challenge, he worried, so she was relieved to see him relaxing with her family.

She narrowed her eyes as he frowned at his phone before tucking it into his pocket. She suspected that it was Tangie trying to get a hold of him. Keisha was still pissed about how everything went down. Tangie was a victim of her father's, and while she knew that, it was hard to reconcile. It had only been a week, and she was still having a hard time with it.

Her mother even more so.

Patrice tried to hide behind the strained smile she wore, but Keisha knew her mother well. It was easy for her to see through the façade. Lucky thought having a family get-together would keep Patrice's mind off of it, but she didn't think it was working. Even now, in the midst of her family, her mother's eyes would dart over to Leland's sisters. Had they known about the child? Keisha was almost afraid to ask, and she was sure Patrice was the same way. Maybe once the sting of betrayal was gone, they could work to get her answers. For now, though, she was leaving well enough alone.

"He's fine," Declan told her, coming up to her at the makeshift bar.

She sighed. "I can feel him, so I know that, but I worry."

"I see why my brother be bossing you around," he told her, giving her another drink. "You worry about everyone around you. That's usually the job he designates for himself."

Keisha sucked her teeth. "Thank you for validating me. I told him that it's not his job to take care of everyone around him."

Declan laughed. "Did you tell yourself that too, shawty?"

"I am not…" She stopped and thought about it. "Whatever, Declan."

He chuckled. "Oh, you funny. It'll be nice to spread some of that worry around. Be even better if you had a couple of kids. Then maybe he'll leave us both alone and focus on them."

She cackled. "Uh-uh, don't be putting kids on me just because your brother be hovering over you."

He chuckled. She sucked her teeth when another one of her cousins came over, making eyes at Declan.

"Girl, carry your ass on somewhere. This man too old for you play with," Keisha snapped at her.

Declan snickered. "It'll be fun having a sister."

Keisha smiled. She didn't grow up with siblings, so having a brother would indeed be fun. The two brothers spent a lot of time together, so she was enjoying getting to know Declan. Thoughts of the brother she'd just discovered threatened to ruin her good mood, but she pushed it aside as a problem for another day.

The rest of the kickback was fun, and even darkness descending didn't stop the partying. It wasn't until Devon shut the music off that people started moving. Keisha laughed because she knew her mother had put him up to it. Her cousins could tell her mother no, but the same couldn't be said for Devon.

An hour later, she was wrapping up cleaning her mother's kitchen, stretching the tightness in her back. She was tired as hell. As she correctly predicted, she handled the bulk of the work while her cousins wrapped to-go plates and scattered. Devon entered the kitchen with the last of the utensils from the grill.

"Food put away. You need anything else, mama?" He leaned down and kissed the top of Patrice's head.

"No, baby. Me and KeKe done in here."

Her wolf moved through her body in contentment. Keisha loved having him in her family unit. They said goodnight to her mother and headed out. Devon grabbed her hand and led her to his truck, helping her inside. Her wolf preened at his careful attention of them. She could understand her animal. She loved the way he cared for her.

She watched him as he drove them home, her hand nestled in his on the middle console. She was fully in love with him and it happened so fast. One moment, she was fighting her mating, and the next, she was breathless and in awe of him. She had been hyper-aware of his every move since they'd been together, watching for any sign that he would be like her father. But so far, he'd done everything he said he'd do, including staying away from his old lifestyle.

Granted, it had only been a few weeks, but she got no indication that Devon planned to play with her heart. He'd been nothing but earnest, from the way he treated her mother to the way he made room for Keisha's independence.

All signs pointed to Devon accepting her the way she was, and she would do the same with him. She'd pushed down on her insecurities, instead embracing their mating, and their bond was tighter for the effort.

He complained about her working too hard, but he never tried to stop her. He moved around her time, never belittling her. It was easy to fall for him. His dominance should've been off-putting, but Devon balanced it in a way that made her wolf want to submit to him wholly.

He lifted their hands and kissed her knuckles.

"I love you," she told him softly.

The smile he gave her had her stomach clenching in lust. "I love you too, mamas."

She knew that they had more challenges ahead of them but she would gladly meet them for him. Devon was everything she never knew she wanted in a mate, and Keisha was thankful that fate had chosen him for her.

Also Available from Dria Andersen

Destiny Series

Destiny Awakened

A Destiny Revealed

Escaping Destiny

Haven Series

Haven

SoulBonded

HellBound

Georgia Arcane Series

Surrender to the Moonlight

Magic in the Moonlight
Fire in the Moonlight

Standalones

Hers to Call

Chasing Savannah

Novellas

Alpha, Lover, Friend

Hamilton Brothers

The Friend Contract

The Alpha's Affair

Porsha's Wolf- A short
Claiming April

Knight Brothers
To Her Rescue
For Her Safety
For Her Peace
For Her Protection

About the Author

I am a full-time photographer and a mom of two. I've been writing my whole life, and after the birth of my first kid, I decided I couldn't very well bring up a fearless human without first trying the things that scared me. So, I wrote my first book and then subsequently more.

I try to write stories I love to read: love stories that feature brown girls like me. Some of my stories feature gods and goddesses and creatures I derived from old African folk tales remixed and thrust into a modern world. Visit my website, www.driaandersen.com, for more information on my other novels.

Join my newsletter for free short stories and more...
www.driaandersen.com